Sequence

by
Kenneth Rogers, Jr.

Rachel,
Thanks for being a
teacher!

Strategic Book Publishing and Rights Co.

Strategic Book Publishing and Rights Co.
12620 FM 1960, Suite A4-507
Houston, TX 77065
www.sbpra.com

ISBN: 978-1-61204-629-7

Design: Dedicated Book Services, Inc. (www.netdbs.com)

For Sarah . . .

Contents

Introduction

I N SIXTH GRADE I FELL IN LOVE WITH THE IDEA OF MY-thology. I can't remember reading any of the stories taught by my English teacher, Mrs. Dye, but I do remember being surprised and excited that all of the gods, demigods, adventures, and characters were considered fact at some point in history. Somewhere in the world, people believed these gods and heroes existed and controlled their lives—until, eventually, they became mere myths, legends, and fables, replaced by proven facts and theories.

A few years ago, I returned to these ancient myths, but rather than ponder whether or not they existed, as I did in sixth grade, I wondered *why* they were created in the first place. Why would a society ever have a need for them then, now, and possibly in the future? And, if these fantastic stories of creation and impossible exploits of ancient heroes *were* ever needed, what would be the state of the world? From these questions, *Sequence* began to take shape—about a world of Clouds that cause unexplainable power outages, electrical storms, the disappearance of wildlife, and the gradual extinction of plant life. The idea of new beginnings in the midst of chaos, explaining the essence of humanity through tragedy, and the exploration of the heavens through the reinforcement of mythology, were the foundations of the story. Just as mythology attempts to explain the origins of mankind from the beginning, *Sequence* uses the experiences and memories of Remus and Charon to describe the range of humanity, what it means to live and love amidst the presence of severe loneliness and depression. *Sequence* begins at the end of humanity and progresses into chaos explaining that as one existence ends another begins.

While reading, remember this: just as Charon and Remus have hidden identities, each of us have our own secrets, lives we conceal and keep separate from the world. Our individuality keeps us alive, safe. When it is exposed, when we are completely vulnerable to those around us, what do we become? And, more importantly, do we have the strength and will to survive?

Pandora

S THE MAN IN BLACK OPENED THE DOOR AND STEPPED through, wind, heat, and sound rushed in behind him. Andrea Remus picked up the small bag beside her foot and followed.

There was no sunlight.

Above, Clouds billowed in and on top of themselves, menacing the sky, radiating heat. In the barren distance, absent of thunder and vegetation, lightning flashed from ground to sky—the only visible light for miles in all directions.

Sweat speckled Andrea's brow. Before wiping it away, moisture evaporated from her skin, cooling her body as the temperature dropped, instantly changing stifling wind to cold breeze. Her fingertips lost feeling.

As they stepped across dry earth to enclosed rocks, the darkened landscape transformed into blackness. Footsteps faltered on loose gravel and dirt as the man in black walked with sure steps toward a gray hatch. Kneeling, he entered five digits before pulling the manhole cover back on its hinges. White light radiated from below, providing definition to the cave and Andrea with light to guide her steps.

The man in black made his way down the stainless steel ladder to a fully lit hall of white incandescent light. Andrea followed, clutching her bag and closing the hatch as she descended. Stepping down, she turned to a hall of seamless white tile, spotless white walls, five steel doors with matching handles, and deafening silence.

The air was still, tepid. Feeling returned to her fingertips.

Two closed doors were on the left, two more on the right, and one straight ahead. The man in black walked to the first on the left and opened it. He spoke: "This is the research room. Inside you will find star maps, tools for calculations, astrological books, magazines, journals, reviews, your own personal notes, and the latest photographs of star systems taken with all spectral lenses. Everything you will need when you are not in direct contact with Pandora will be located in this room."

Closing the door, the man in black stepped across the hall, his footfall filling the complex with sound, and opened a second door, revealing a single bed, desk, lamp, small closet, dresser, mirror, shower, and drain separated from the room by a plastic curtain, and an overhead light that flickered to life when they entered.

"This will be your room. As you can see, living arrangements have been dictated by current changes. Besides the shower, the layout is the same for both rooms. Because of the need to conserve energy and resources, we could only have one installed. As before, it is on a fifteen-minute timer that can only be set and used twice daily." Without another word, the man in black walked to the door next to Andrea's.

Before closing the door, she placed her bag on the glossy floor and followed him toward what she remembered to be the kitchen.

"There is no refrigerator. The door on the right wall gives access to the pantry, which contains all the dry foods you'll need. There is a stove, and kitchen accessories are in the cupboards. Like the shower, the sink is set to dispense two gallons of water a day and the stove can only be used for two hours. There's no washer or dryer. To wash your clothes, include it in your water usage from day to day, or use bottled water."

The man in black walked to the back wall of the kitchen, continuing to speak. "Trash can be put here." He pulled back a slot that blended seamlessly into the white wall. "It leads to an incinerator lit once a week."

The man in the black suit closed the slot, walked past Andrea and out of the kitchen toward the control room. There was no label to distinguish it from the other rooms.

Inside were three screens that wrapped from one side of the room to the other, filling the entire back wall. Displayed were three separate images. To the left was a detailed diagram of the solar system, showing the planets, known meteors, and comets moving in their orbits around the Sun, filling the screen with vivid color. The screen to the right was a halo of frozen comets outlying the 5.9-trillion-mile graviton radius of the solar system's Sun. And the center screen showed a spiraling galaxy of dazzling yellows, purples, blues, and blacks as they rotated in sync around a glowing center.

Seeing the screens, Andrea began feeling anxious.

Below the screens was a single computer console, with two monitors and keyboards on either side and a clock in the center, the only one in the facility, displaying the time, day, month, and year in black lettering on a green background.

Sitting in the chair to the left, staring into his monitor, was the haggard image of Thomas Charon.

He turned from his monitor with an expression of horror and surprise on his unshaven face. Realizing who the two individuals were and why they were there, fear dissolved from his features.

The man in black continued to address Andrea. "This will be your connection to Pandora. To the right is a display of the Oort Cloud—"

"Hello, Andrea—it's been a long time."

Thomas stared at the profile of the woman before him, studying the new wrinkles and lines of her face since their last meeting twelve years prior. Andrea's eyes remained transfixed on the spiraling galaxy. The man in black attempted to continue, but Thomas cut him off.

"I think we can take it from here, Munin. This isn't our first rodeo."

Munin, the man in black, turned and walked toward the open door. Before leaving, he turned and spoke. "Dr. Charon, you have all the information for Dr. Remus. See to it she receives it. The terms of the agreement are the same as before. Besides living arrangements, nothing has changed. Our data shows the Pandora operating systems are the same as before. There should be no problems. We look forward to hearing from you both, soon. Good luck."

With that said, Munin turned and walked down the hall and climbed up the ladder into the raging storm above. The closing lid echoed throughout the hall.

Andrea and Thomas were alone. Electricity filled the empty space.

He attempted to sound pleasant, but exhaustion came through in his voice. "So? How have you been? Do you enjoy teaching high school students, or is it more frustrating than configuring orbital equations?"

Rather than answer, Andrea asked questions of her own. "You haven't been sleeping?"

Her eyes remained focused on the screen ahead. Thomas shifted his weight. He looked toward the ground.

"How long have you been here?" she asked.

"Not sure. It's hard to keep track. You know how it is."

He looked into Andrea's face. She wouldn't meet his gaze. "I wanted to check out the system. Make sure everything was working properly before you arrived. I figured it would be best to limit your exposure."

"Only mine?" Andrea turned from the screen to Thomas. Both could feel the tension that had not dissipated since their last meeting. Andrea shifted her attention to the task before them and her eyes back to the screens.

"The Outages have gotten worse—much worse than I think anyone planned. It's projected to continue."

"How long do we have?" she asked.

"As long as we need."

"Or as much as we can handle.

Both knew she was right.

"Have you seen her?"

It was a question Thomas was prepared to answer honestly. "Yes."

"So nothing has changed?"

Thomas paused, questioning whether he should tell her now, or wait. He knew he would have to eventually, if she did not discover it on her own. "Not from what I can tell."

With a heavy sigh and a cluttered mind, Andrea said, "What's the destination? Is it still Gliese, or has it changed?"

Thomas would not meet her gaze. Instead he turned to his monitor and picked up a manila folder marked with the word "Pandora" in bold print. He handed it to Andrea.

Andrea's expression became stern when she looked at its contents. "HD? Epsilon? Kappa? There are eighteen planets on this list."

Thomas said nothing.

"The compositions of most of these are unknown. What's the point of sending data if they can't support life?" She closed the folder with disdain. Thomas sat in the chair, not knowing what to say.

"You know how long it took me last time. And Gliese was a quarter of the distance. It's been twelve years, Tom. I haven't done any major calculations—I've been teaching high school English."

Andrea shook her head, her eyes on the ground. "It'll take too long. I can't do it."

"What choice do we have?"

Frustrated, annoyed, Andrea turned and walked toward the door and the empty white hall. "Try to get some sleep," she said without looking back.

"Andrea?"

She stopped, but did not turn.

"If you need me tonight . . . for anything—"

"Thanks, Tom, but I'm sure you'll have your own demons to face."

Thomas watched as she walked down the hall and into her room. Sitting there, silent, he thought of the storm raging above, affecting every aspect of their lives. As he looked at the Pandora's screens, sunlight shined down from a corner of the room. It grew in intensity, blinding his vision before fading, allowing sight to return.

In place of screens he was seeing a window that revealed sunlight and leafless trees. Instead of a computer and monitors, there was a kitchen table. Dish soap and the scent of lavender filled the room. Cupboards, dishes, utensils, and appliances lined the walls and filled drawers, replacing flashing lights and rotating chairs. Thomas saw the image of his father in running shoes, shorts, and shirt pass the window toward the suburban street.

Parked in the driveway was a fully assembled black motorcycle with orange waves lining its frame. Thomas admired its craftsmanship, then called to his mother, who materialized before the sink, washing the lunch dishes.

"Mom? Where's Dad going?"

"For a run."

"What's he running from?"

The woman smiled. "He's not running from anything, Sweetheart. He's exercising. He likes to stay in shape by running through parts of the neighborhood. It helps him stay strong."

"How far does he go?" Thomas asked.

"About five miles."

"By himself?" Thomas asked in amazement.

The woman shook her head, continuing to smile.

Surprised by his father's physical endurance, Thomas turned in his chair. Sunlight faded. The window vanished. Visions of his mother and father dispersed, along with the happiness. Computers returned, screens appeared, and sadness lingered.

Thomas moved his hand across his face, clearing away thoughts. Instead, he just wiped away sweat. Breathing deeply, he studied his monitor. Another memory appeared, waiting to be analyzed and loaded. Looking away, he made his way toward the door and his room. Entering, he closed the door, went to his desk, picked up the tape recorder, and began to speak.

"I saw my parents. It was the day I . . ."

Thomas paused, letting emotions drain before continuing.

"The replays are growing stronger, more vivid. The stronger the relationship I build with the device, the more frequent and longer the flashes occur. As was reported by Dr. Remus and myself twelve years prior, the flashes only occur when we're not working in direct contact with Pandora. However, this may not be the case. To try and minimize its effects, I've decided to try a different method than before. Rather than working on Pandora in small intervals, building toward longer and more intense occurrences, I'm working on the machine as much as possible in an attempt to keep my memories from jumping from one time frame to the next. So far it has worked, but there—"

Thinking he heard something from the hall, he lowered the recorder. As he did, the sound faded. Concentrating, Thomas continued. ". . . but there have been instances. It's growing harder to pull myself from the past. So far I've had fourteen replays—all different. I have reason to believe our previous work on Pandora is a factor. Dr. Remus arrived today—"

The sound of voices on the other side of the door began to fill the room. Trying his best to ignore them, he finished his report as best he could. "I'm not certain how long it will take Andrea to make the calculations, but our minds were tested to take months of Pandora's effects. At least, they used to. I'm not so sure anymore."

Thomas took a breath before continuing, allowing time to process his thoughts. "There's always a connection. I just have to find it."

He turned off the recorder and placed it on the desk, then walked to the door. The voices had grown too loud to ignore. Grasping the handle, taking a deep breath, he prepared himself for what he was about to see. He opened the door to rushing teenagers heading out of the school building toward buses and cars. Down the hall was Melissa Pomene.

"Hey, Mel!" Thomas yelled.

Melissa smiled. "Hey, Tom. I see you're ready for practice." Thomas looked down to see shorts and running shoes. He leaned against the locker beside Melissa's.

"What does coach Hertzsprung have you CC boys doing today?"

"Hill work, I think. But you never know. Could be quarters, half-mile intervals, maybe even a time trial. You never know."

"Wow. You make it sound so exciting."

"What can I say? It's a gift. You ladies have a game today, right?"

"Yup."

"Nervous?"

"Yup."

"Really? I thought you got over your nervousness about games last year."

"I did, but that was when I was playing as a freshman. Today I'm playing varsity."

"Varsity? Congrats, Kid! You deserve it. First time?"

Melissa nodded.

"Don't be nervous. I've seen you play. You're great."

"I'm good, not great."

"Good enough to make varsity as a sophomore."

Melissa gave him a fresh smile as she pulled her bag out of her locker and began loading it with textbooks. "Thanks, but some of us do feel pressure. We all can't excel without even trying."

"I try—"

"When was the first time you were put on varsity? Freshman year?"

A smile was his only reply.

"I thought so. Not only do I have the game tonight, but a geometry test tomorrow, and pages to read for Mr. Haley's class. I don't even want to think about there being an Outage tonight."

"You'll get through it. Just focus on one thing at a time. That's what I do."

"Really? I thought you got straight As without even picking up a book."

Closing the locker, Melissa made her way down the now deserted hallway. Thomas walked beside her. "For your information," he said, "I did pick up a book—once."

"I hope I can say that my senior year. Then she changed the subject. "How's your dad?"

The smile dissolved from Thomas's face. "He's hanging in there. The headaches are getting worse, but he's got most of the motorcycle put back together."

"Well, remember—my window is always open."

"Thanks." The smile reappeared on Thomas's face. Down the hall, other boys in shorts began making their way toward them.

"Here come your buddies—Hooligans, or whatever you call yourselves these days."

"This year we're the Outcasts."

"Is there a reason?"

"Because we do better than the football team and get no recognition."

"That's a pretty good reason."

Without saying a word, two of the four boys grabbed Thomas beneath the arms and lifted him from the ground. He didn't struggle. The smile remained on his face.

"Sorry, Mel—we need to borrow him for a bit. You can have him back later," one of the boys said.

"Keep him. I don't want him anymore." Melissa watched as they carried Thomas away.

"Aww, that hurts," he called over his shoulder. "But I still love you. And don't worry about the game—you'll do great. I'll see you tomorrow!"

"I don't see why you two just don't date," another of the boys said as they put Thomas back on the ground.

"Who?" Thomas asked. "Mel and me? We're just friends. And besides, she's a sophomore."

Melissa Pomene gave a final wave and a smile before turning toward the girls' locker room. Thomas watched as the high school hall faded and the door to the control room reappeared. Shaking his head, he returned to his room, closed the door, and sat on the edge of his bed.

Staring at his feet, Thomas was trying to relax his mind when he heard the voice of his freshman history teacher and high school football coach, Henry Russell, getting louder. The sound filled the room, blinding his vision as pain pulsated in his head. He closed his eyes, hoping that would block Russell's droning voice. When he opened his eyes, he saw his room was filled with twenty classmates, friends, posters and art depicting aspects of world history, papers, notes, and a chalkboard filled with notes. Mr. Russell called his name from the front of the room. In his hand was a call slip.

"Tom, you're needed in the office."

Standing from his desk, Thomas retrieved his books from beneath his desk, stepped toward the door, and walked out the Enriched History class to the school office. When he walked in, his smile was greeted by the secretary's somber expression.

"Tom, gather your things and meet your mother in the front of the building in five minutes. Here's a hall pass."

"What's this about?"

"I can't . . ." She tripped over her words, unsure of how to respond. "She'll tell you when she gets here. Hurry—she'll be here soon."

Thomas took the pass and headed toward the door as the school bell rang, startling him to the present emptiness of his room as he sat on the edge of the stiff mattress of his bed.

Breathing heavily, sweat dripping from his chin, Thomas was unable to shake the fear washing over him. Pain pulsed in his head. Standing, he removed his clothing, exposing his skin to the slightly cooler air. He put on a robe, grabbed his shower supplies, and made his way to Andrea's room.

He knocked twice. Receiving no response, he opened the door. Andrea was sitting at her desk, her back to him, reading.

Thomas stepped into the shower and closed the curtain, then took off his robe and put his shower kit on the floor. He turned the faucet and let the tepid water run down his head and over his body, the feeling on his eyes and face calming his nerves.

Thomas heard nothing from Andrea on the other side of the curtain. He was completely immersed in the few moments of relief Pandora had allowed him before again sending him back to the past. Fearful of letting his mind wander, he focused on the water and nothing else. He didn't think of Pandora, the storm raging out of control above, or the woman on the other side of the shower curtain reading Roman mythology.

Thomas did not turn off the water. He let it run before it shut off on its own after its fifteen-minute allotment was used up, leaving him naked and wet, his eyes closed and head down. Concentrating on the movement of air in and out of his lungs as water dripped from his body to the drain, he attempted to regain his composure.

Putting on his robe and picking up the kit he didn't use, Thomas pulled back the curtain to reveal the naked body of Andrea Remus.

She did not move. She stood in the middle of the room, looking into Thomas's eyes with a distant expression and the sad eyes he remembered from twelve years ago. They stood looking at the other, waiting to move or speak, when a name Thomas didn't mean to say escaped his lips.

"Melissa—I . . ."

As the name came and went, Thomas knew his mistake. Breaking the trance, Andrea walked to her bed, dropped on top of the white linen sheets, and stared into the wall.

Her back remained bare and exposed. "Leave," was all she said, and needed to say.

Thomas left her room and went to his own. She continued to stare at the wall as the cool air of the complex rose bringing goose bumps to her naked skin when suddenly the weight of 210 fully clothed pounds caused Andrea to gasp. Silent tears rolled from eyes that now saw a bedroom ceiling speckled with the glow-in-the-dark neon green stars her brother, Michael, had helped her put up years ago. Slow, heavy breathing was muffled by the pillow under her head. Andrea lay still, counting the moments. Feeling the middle-aged man's pace increase, she braced herself for what was to come.

Slow moans of pleasure began to rise deep inside Daryl Tyr's chest as he pushed harder and faster. Andrea, sheets balled in her hands, held back groans of pain. With a final release, Daryl let his body relax.

Andrea remained stiff and tense.

Daryl's heavy breathing and full weight forced Andrea to lie still. She concentrated on the ceiling and not on the hairy forearm pressed against the side of her face.

Daryl lifted himself from the girl's body, closed the bedroom door, crept to Evelyn Remus Tyr's room, and slipped in beside the still form of his wife, Andrea's mother.

Andrea did not move. She remained motionless, staring at the ceiling. Outside, black Clouds blanketed the night sky, hiding the stars.

Tears ran down her face into her pillow as the slow hum of Pandora circulated throughout the room.

Something had changed.

✳ ✳ ✳

Thomas opened the door to the white-lit kitchen to see Andrea sitting at the small circular table opposite, drinking a cup of coffee. Closing the door, Thomas pulled the only other mug from the cupboard and poured a cup for himself. He leaned against the counter behind the woman.

The only sound in the sterile room was the electricity humming through lights above their heads from three magnetic generators buried beneath their feet. In a place where silence filled time and space, a moment could feel like an hour, and sound was a necessity.

"Couldn't sleep?" Thomas asked, eager to fill the void.

"I guess you could say that." Andrea stared into the contents of her cup.

"No caramel milk?"

"All we have is powdered. Doesn't taste the same," Andrea responded, keeping her head and eyes focused on the contents of the cup.

Thomas shook his head, taking a sip of his own coffee.

Both sat silently, pondering their thoughts. Thomas felt obliged to show Andrea what he'd discovered, knowing he should, but moments before opening his mouth to speak, he decided against it. Instead he attempted to explain, as simply as he could, what he believed needed to be done to ensure the completion of their mission—and, hopefully, their survival.

"Andrea, I think we need a different approach than before."

There was a pause before she responded. Then, "And what would that be?"

Thomas cleared his throat before continuing, unsure how she would react. "Sharing the memories."

Andrea paused again, studying her cup. "What do you mean, share? We both know that's impossible."

Eager to share his new findings, Thomas left the counter-top and took the seat opposite her. He leaned forward and began. "There's the possibility that two individuals, trans-mitting the same frequency, can have the same memory at the same time."

"Munin never mentioned this."

"Munin doesn't know. No one does."

"And how do you? The memories are completely random."

"It's difficult, but the connection can be made. It hap-pened to us."

They looked at each other, each knowing what the other was thinking.

He went on. "All it requires is two individuals giving off the same brain frequency when recalling a memory. This means the two individuals have to be so well connected, so attuned to the other, that Pandora only recognizes and re-plays one memory."

Andrea said nothing—she just stared at the cold contents of her cup before drinking the dregs. Thomas watched with-out speaking. Then she got up and placed her cup in the empty sink. Her face remained expressionless.

"I'm going to spend the day in the research room before beginning work from the control room," she said. "I suggest you get some rest." She turned from the sink and walked toward the door.

"Andrea, if we're going to get through this we have to . . . Andrea?"

The door closed, leaving Thomas alone beneath the white lights. Emptying his cup into the sink, he put it beside Andrea's and went to his room to take a stab at sleep.

✳ ✳ ✳

Andrea counted the seconds. Afraid to let her mind slip to any specific memory, she laid still, her eyes closed in hopes it would fool her brain into shutting itself down.

After moments of silence, Andrea opened her eyes to a black sky, the smell of wood, dust, the sound of footsteps coming up the attic stairs of her childhood home, and the sight of distant stars and planets through a refracting telescope lens.

A small smile spread across her young face.

"Andrea? You up here?" Michael Balder Remus whispered from the stairs.

Peeking through the thin rails of the banister, he looked into the shadows to see the outline of his sister near the open attic window, bent over a telescope. He rubbed his shoulders for warmth. He saw the white fog of his breath. "Why is it so cold?" he asked.

"The temperature dropped and hasn't risen since the Outage. Did you know the Clouds look exactly like the night sky, just without stars or a moon? It's like . . . space."

"Do you know what time it is?" Michael asked, coming up the last of the steps and turning the corner. "Are you even able to see anything through that . . . thing?"

As if deep in thought, perhaps studying an object of interest deep in the night sky, Andrea answered her brother slowly. "The Cloud passed hours ago. Besides, this is the best time of night to see Callisto."

"At two-thirty in the morning? How do you know all of this?"

"I read."

"You're nine."

"So? I'm not allowed to read?"

"No—it's just . . . weird. But still cool," Michael said with a smile. "However, that still doesn't change the fact that you should be in bed before ten."

"And it still doesn't change the fact that you said you would be home two-and–a-half hours ago. You know, if Mom found out you left me here alone at night while she was at work instead of babysitting, she wouldn't be very happy with you," Andrea said, looking up from the telescope.

"She would be more upset if I took you with me. Besides, the car wouldn't start."

"The Outage as been over for three hours. And it was just a small Cloud."

"It's more than just a Cloud."

"You still should have been home sooner."

"Good point," he agreed. "Tell you what—I'll make you a deal. I won't tell Mom you were up here after I put you to bed if you don't tell her I went out and left you alone."

"Do I ever?"

He smiled. "I guess not." Taking her by the shoulders, he lifted her head from the single ocular lens and steered her toward the stairs. "Come on, Kid. Stop working for the night and go to bed before Mom gets home and we both get in trouble. I think you forget how old you are sometimes."

"How can I forget when you keep reminding me?"

As he guided her down the attic steps, she blinked, and was back in the stagnant air of the bunker. She felt twenty years older; mentally and emotionally. The smile washed from her face as her eyes and mind refocused on the ceiling.

Down the hall, behind a closed door, Thomas's thoughts drifted from the confines of his sterile white room to a bright blue sky of white clouds. Skyscrapers towering over his out-stretched body raced by as he lay in the bed of a moving pickup truck. From his position, he could hear the sound of moving vehicles and the laughter of Mel Pomene from the open window above his head as she sang along to the radio with Rita Leavitt. Thomas could feel Melissa's gaze, but, for the moment, his mind was focused on the clouds overhead and the space beyond.

"Stay still," Melissa whispered to Thomas from the passenger side of the truck. "A cop just pulled up."

He nodded. The truck came to a stop at an intersection, causing his body to slide forward. Melissa stared down into his face. Looking over his head, he caught her round eyes and upside-down smile. Looking up, he couldn't help but think how beautiful she was.

"Hold on," the girl whispered low enough for only Thomas to hear.

When the truck moved, momentum forced his body to slide away from Melissa's slender cheeks and light red hair to the back of the bed, where his feet came to rest against the tailgate. Thomas's attention went back to the sky, the clouds, and the sculpted moldings on the side of historic buildings looming overhead. Looking up, he felt a sense of relief he had not felt since his father's death. He closed his eyes and felt the wind move across his body, making him believe he was flying aimlessly through the afternoon sky while at the same moment, in a different room of the Pandora Complex, Andrea's young hand felt the worn leather of Michael's steering wheel beneath her palms.

"Okay. Now what do you do?" Michael asked.

"I don't know," she said, gripping the wheel, looking around in confusion. "Hit the gas?"

"No—I'm taking care of the gas, the clutch, and the brake. You take care of the driving. So what do you do?"

Andrea said nothing as the car slowed down a neighboring side street of dormant lawns, dead plants, absent animals, and partially leafless trees.

"You know when it's the best time of night to see the Collisto constellation, but you can't tell me what to do next when driving a stick shift?"

"It's *Callisto*, not Collisto—a moon of Saturn, and I'm only nine. How am I supposed to know how to drive a car?"

"So, *now* you're nine?" Michael asked, chuckling.

"Mike!"

"Okay, okay. You have to change gears. We can't stay in first all day."

"Which gear do I put it in?" she asked, glancing down at the gear shift. "This one?"

Looking down at her hand, Michael panicked.

"No—second! Second! Down!"

"Down?"

"Yes—down!"

With more force than usual, the car kicked into second gear and picked up speed, running more smoothly.

"Now put it in third," he said, a bit more calmly.

"This one?" she asked, pointing to the middle gear, taking her eyes off the road.

"Yup. And don't forget to steer."

"Got it," Andrea said, looking back at the road, both hands on the wheel. "This is easy."

Michael laughed. "That's because you're doing the *easy part*."

"Easy part? I just changed the gears. What did you do? Keep your foot on the gas? Either way, I think I would be fine if I were doing this on my own."

"You probably would be if your feet could reach the accelerator, brake, *and* clutch."

"Minor details." Focusing on the road, Andrea shifted into fourth.

Michael gave another laugh and agreed. "You're right. You *would* be fine on your own."

Andrea moved her hand from the gear shift of the past to the side of her desk in the present in a desperate attempt to ground herself, and her thoughts. Rather than fight the impact of reborn memories, as Andrea was trying to do, Thomas was giving in completely to Pandora's effects, his mind in the past. Taking no notice of the sheets and mattress under his body, the truck he felt instead began to slow as it bounced over speed bumps before coming to a stop.

He opened his eyes but did not move. Instead, he looked at the few leaves on the branches overhead. He listened as the truck's engine shut off, then heard both doors open and close. When the tailgate was dropped, Thomas looked to his right and saw Melissa resting her chin on her hands on the side of the truck. Looking at her, he could not help but smile in return. He sat up and looked out over the somewhat deserted city park.

To the right was a pond of semi-transparent greenish water. Parents with strollers, kids with pets, and loving couples populated its shore. Conversations were the only sounds in the spring air due to the recent, absence of animals and insects. Overhead, Thomas could hear bare branches clacking against one another in the wind.

The day was growing late.

As the Sun set, Thomas felt the cool breeze against his skin. Melissa's short hair blew across her face, and she tucked it behind her right ear.

Comfort and security washed over Thomas in Melissa's presence, but Andrea was left feeling half alive, bleeding, and alone on the brightly lit street of her home town that was lined with stores decorated for Christmas. Adrenaline propelled feelings of sadness, confusion, and horror throughout her body as images of her brother's dying body, and smell of oxygen-poor blood flooded her mind and senses, one after the other.

She began to scream. "Micky! Wake up, Mike! *Mike*!"

Looking out over the deserted street, Andrea looked for anyone who could help, but they were all in their homes, away from the approaching threat looming overhead, blackening the night sky. "Someone help—*please!*"

In a pool of oil, gas, blood, and broken glass, Andrea grabbed her brother's body and pulled it close to her own. She continued to cry for help from the middle of the intersection as lightning soundlessly reached from ground to sky and the temperature dropped quickly. Her tears fell onto her brother's body as the sound of her voice echoed off the enclosed walls of her room inside the Pandora Complex. Feelings of panic, fear, and hatred for the black, lifeless old sky outside the complex remained fresh in her mind.

Frustrated, exhausted, and upset, she walked to her door and opened it just as Thomas Charon asked Mel Pomene what they were going to do in City Park. Melissa looked at Rita, then back to Thomas. Before answering, there were two knocks on the steel door of his room. He opened his eyes. Sitting up in bed, he was startled back to reality.

Andrea opened the door and poked her head inside. "I can't sleep. You ready to get started?"

Half conscious, Thomas nodded, his face glistening with sweat. He could feel the moisture on his skin under his clothes, wiping out his feeling of security and replacing it with discomfort.

"You okay?" she asked.

"Yeah," he responded. "Just give me a second to get myself together and I'll be fine. Are you okay? I thought you were going to spend the day in the research room."

Andrea considered telling him of the memory replays that had occurred without being in contact with the Pandora computer system, but decided against it. "I changed my mind. I'll meet you in the room."

As Andrea walked toward her work station, Thomas swung his feet across the side of the bed, picked up the recorder, and began to speak. "It's getting worse . . ." Two drops of blood fell from his nose to the recorder.

❋ ❋ ❋

Thomas closed the door, then began pacing from one side of the room to the other. His hands shook as his steps faltered.

He forced his attention to the ground, feeling too many racing thoughts to make sense of them all. Frustrated, he went to the side of his desk, picked up the recorder again, and began speaking into the microphone.

"Things are worse than originally anticipated—much worse. It's only been one day, and Pandora has copied numerous memories from Andrea. I hoped I was wrong in my assumptions, but I now know I was correct. Andrea needs to know. I have to show her the list before the replays become too difficult to handle. I hope she understands why I made the agreement with Munin. Either way, we're trapped until the courses are plotted and the spectrum of emotions are completely filled. Until then, there's nothing else we can do."

Thomas shut off the recorder, placed it on his desk, and walked out his door to Andrea's room. He stood outside her door, then, nervously, knocked twice.

"Andrea? We need to talk. It's about the replays. Something's changed, and . . ."

There was no response.

"Andrea?"

He stood, silently, waiting, but heard no sound from inside Andrea's room, even as her mind wandered to late August, the midday sun beating down from a clear blue sky to a bright yellow taxi.

Pandora began to copy the memory to its files—Andrea sitting alone in the cab, waiting for standstill traffic to gain enough momentum to reach the traffic light ahead, the one that kept changing from green to yellow to red. But tires remained still.

Extending in front of the yellow cab was a line of gleaming windshields and heated exteriors of loaded SUVs and minivans that extended through the light, down the main drag, and onto every side street and parking lot of the university.

To the right, past the metal guard rail and dying prairie grass, was the university football stadium. No words of inspiration were displayed on its walls or on banners draped from rafters. All she could see from her back seat were brown cement columns extending upward from the ground, each holding the weight of empty stairs and vacant seats.

All was quiet, still. There was no movement, no hint of human activity. From Andrea's cushioned sanctuary, it was alien in appearance.

The taxi began to inch forward.

Rather than focus on the stadium and parking lot moving along the back window, Andrea looked to the bustling activities of gas stations, restaurants, and hotels as the taxi made a right onto Main toward the campus. Parents, students, and children all moved from their cars to one location or another. All were in a hurry.

Reports circulated. A Cloud had been spotted in the distance.

Her eyes couldn't stay on the strangers for long. Instead she studied the yellow and white lines on the road as her mind drifted to thoughts of fear, worry, and a rapidly approaching future. Her body gently swayed back and forth with each stop and start of the cab as it passed through intersections and jammed parking lots before coming to a stop near the back entrance of the dorm where she would spend the rest of her academic year—McConklin Hall.

The driver put the car in park, then got out and walked to the trunk and removed Andrea's only possession—a blue plywood trunk with gold latches.

Andrea stepped out of the backseat, paid the driver, and watched as the taxi pulled away, eager to escape. He would not make it back before the Outage.

As the sound of its engine mingled with the noise of moving bodies and chaos, Andrea watched the movements of other incoming freshmen. In every direction, car and truck doors swung open. Men and women, boys and girls moved clothing and moving bins filled with electronics and other personal belongs to closets and shelves in rooms they'd call home for the next nine months.

Sweat, exhaustion, and worry were on every face . All were excited and afraid. Andrea couldn't help wondering why. What made them so happy? What made them different from herself?

No answers came as she stood near the side of the building that was her residence hall.

Andrea was ignored in the sea of moving bodies as she made her way to the back doors of the building, leaving her trunk alone and unattended.

Walking down the steps of the carpeted freshman dormitory lobby, she tried as best she could to maneuver around sidesteps and shuffles of individuals waiting for the packed elevator that led to their floor. Andrea inspected the layout of the dormitory.

Beneath her feet was green carpet, trampled by constant foot traffic. In front was a pillar of fluorescent light, which illuminated the front desk and the surrounding area. Behind were closed doors to offices, and in front, a hall curved toward the side exit.

Holding the key to her room, Andrea walking to the side of the desk, found a dolly, and began maneuvering through the crowded lobby to the trunk she left unattended.

With little difficulty, Andrea was able to load the beaten trunk and move it from the parking lot to the air-conditioned interior of the building, where she waited with other newly arriving freshmen and their families for a place on the overcrowded elevator.

As she stood there, she studied the expressions and moods of individuals around the elevator doors, listening to side conversations, complaints about heat exhaustion, hunger, thirst, fear of the approaching Outage.

Thoughts and memories of the past flashed through her mind out of sequence, confusing themselves with abstract thoughts of imaginative daydreams and sacrilegious nightmares.

The doors slid open. Students and parents exited, allowing Andrea and others to enter.

At the chime of a bell and the flash of red light from illuminated numbers above, Andrea pushed the loaded dolly out of the elevator and into the hall, then to the right. She passed the open doors of female teenagers.

As she moved past room after room, it struck her that each open door was like a single frame on a movie reel. Each person in each room was assembling pieces of furniture, putting away clothing and accessories, or making bonds of friendship. Microwaves and portable fans were placed on stands and in corners. Personal furnishings were added to the decor. Posters and pictures were hung on white walls. Stereos and

alarm clocks were plugged in. All were happy with themselves and one another as they moved through the scenes of
their lives.

Andrea stopped and stood at the closed door of room 327.
Standing the dolly aside, she took the key from her pocket
and opened the door.

Inside, the room was bright with sunshine from open windows. Beneath the lofted wooden-framed bed was a single
chair, television stand, and thirteen–inch TV. From the open
window she heard nothing from the previously crowded
street below, only the faint sound of distant Sirens. She
flipped the light switch. The Sirens eerily silenced, but nothing else happened as the Sun shined on.

Andrea stepped into the hall and maneuvered the trunk
across the gray and blue carpet into her room. She shut the
door, then eased the dolly out from under the blue plywood
trunk. Then she opened three gold latches and lifted the lid.
Reaching inside, she pulled out three identical pairs of jeans,
five shirts, twelve pairs of underwear, eight bras, and one
jacket. The only remaining items were living necessities:
books on Roman mythology, notes and calculations of astronomy she had collected over the years, scientific magazines
dating back more than twelve years, and a pair of binoculars.

There were no posters of dream destinations, pictures
of friends who went to distant colleges promising to stay
in touch, or family members she would see at Thanksgiving and Christmas. There was only a lime green towel, two
sheets, and a thin comforter.

She picked up her belongings and put them where they
belonged on her side of the room. Her clothing went into the
dresser, leaving the closet empty. The single towel went onto
the towel rack beside the door. The two sheets and comforter
went over the mattress. Books, magazines, and notes were
placed on the desktop bookshelf, and the binoculars went in
the bottom drawer of the desk.

Looking over the room that was now partially her own,
she felt no connection to her surroundings. Andrea decided

to leave. She grabbed the dolly, opened the door, and went into the empty hall. Locking the door behind her, she headed toward the stairs, passing closed door after closed door.

Leaving the dolly beside the deserted desk, Andrea walked through the lobby exit into the silence of the now deserted city. There was no wind.

Car doors hung open on their hinges. Clothing was left in piles by adolescent boys and girls along the sidewalk. Bins of electronics and personal items were left unattended.

The temperature cooled, dropping steadily toward freezing.

Passing vacated vehicles, Andrea made her way to the heart of campus. All was silent and still. She focused on the sound of her worn shoes as they hit the pavement.

The sidewalk continued.

Shadows of overhanging tree branches, bare of leaves since early July, were cast from above. Hills of faded grass, silent dormitories, classrooms, and dining halls were on either side of the single-lane street. The Sun continued to shine from a perfect blue sky, but the air felt like ice on her skin.

The sidewalk ended.

In an open field of faded green grass was the campus observatory. In the distance, beyond the field, was the highway, and a line of engine dead vehicles. In the sky was a single, small jet-black Cloud.

It approached.

Andrea made her way into the observatory as lightning flashed from sky to ground in the distance. There was no thunder.

✳ ✳ ✳

As Pandora downloaded memories from Andrea's past, Thomas opened the door to her room.

Andrea sat on the floor beside her bed, shattered glass in hand, blood leaking from exposed wrists.

Pandora continued to copy memories from Andrea as she turned the worn handle, opening the door to the unfurnished studio apartment in the past.

Inside were white barren walls and a gray carpet. She grabbed the black plastic handle of the blue plywood trunk and dragged it across the gray and white linoleum to the living room rug. On the other side of the door, in the dingy, smoky hall, she picked up the remainder of her possessions. Closing the door, she looked over the bleak apartment.

To the right was a wooden-handled, outdated cream-colored refrigerator. Opening both doors, she inhaled the stale air, captive for weeks, now allowed to escape.

Rusted metal racks held a single empty ice tray.

Closing its doors, Andrea stepped behind the refrigerator, pushed the two-pronged plug into the three-pronged outlet, and listened as the ancient wiring crackled to life.

A few inches away was a sink of dull stainless steel and sparse countertops. Cupboards were the same glossy finish as the door to the apartment. Stove burners were rusted, and the countertop was the same creamy color as the refrigerator. Thick plastic curtains covered two partially open windows.

Parting the curtains, Andrea felt the cracked plastic beneath her fingertips.

Sunlight and the sound of dwindling traffic entered the room with ease through the windows. Below, people moved quickly from one store to the next, buying goods from locally owned and operated businesses. In the distant sky, a single black Cloud, much larger than ones in the past, moved against the wind toward the city.

Cars parked on the side of the road would not be moved for the rest of the night.

After gazing absently at the brick walls and sculpted moldings of downtown buildings, she stepped away from the windows to the trunk and opened the three latches.

Rearranging books of Roman mythology, astronomy, and advanced trigonometry, Andrea removed a single towel and went to her bathroom. Shutting the door, she went to the tub and turned on the shower. There was no curtain.

Andrea focused on undoing the buttons of her jeans, removing her shirt and socks and throwing them to the floor, along with the towel. Without testing the temperature of the water, Andrea stepped under the showerhead, letting the drops run down her face to her body, spattering water onto the bathroom floor.

There was no soap. The water pressure was low. The temperature was tepid.

The streams of water coursing over her face and down her body to the drain were enough to ease her mind for a few moments. With her hands at her sides, she could hear Sirens just as the water shut off and the lights went out.

In the dark, alone and wet, Andrea let the last few drops of water drip from her body before opening her eyes to darkness. Carefully stepping out of the shower, she searched the floor for her towel. Finding it, she did not wrap it around her body. Instead she held it in her hand as she opened the bathroom door to a bleak room, completely absent of sunlight and the sounds of passing cars from the street below.

Downtown streets and shops were deserted. The black Cloud was visible.

Dripping water, Andrea left her clothing on the wet bathroom floor. She stepped to the trunk in the center of the dimly lit room and removed a single pair of socks, a blanket and a pillow. She unfolded the blanket and sat beneath the open curtains.

Drying off and putting on socks, Andrea spread out the blanket on the carpet, laid down, and slept in the darkness of her empty apartment as flashes of static electricity flickered outside the window . There was no wind.

The Cloud remained stationary as the temperature steadily dropped.

Hours later, Andrea awoke to a clear sky, cold air, and bright street lamps shining through the frosty window. Gray shadows sulked in each corner of the empty apartment.

Andrea lay on the carpet, quiet, eyes wide, the blanket pulled over her shoulders. Focusing, she was able to distinguish the large, elongated shape that was her brother's trunk, and the two black holes that were her open closet and bathroom door.

The streets were still silent as late night became early morning.

Standing up, Andrea let the blanket slip to the carpet as she walked to the trunk. The air was cool against her skin as she knelt down and lifted the lid back on its hinges. Removing the last remaining books of mythology, astronomy, and meager clothing, she then pulled out the carefully wrapped binoculars, setting them carefully on the floor. Quickly putting on a pair of sweatpants and short-sleeved shirt, she picked up the binoculars and walked out her apartment door towards the night sky.

Andrea walked down the silent hall of the apartment building to the back entrance, opened the door, and stepped onto the steel scaffolding into cool summer air. The rising temperature of the night air overtook the smell of stale smoke.

Descending from the upper level apartments was a metal fire escape that reached the first floor and connected to the businesses below. Instead of going down to the world where she felt disconnected, she climbed the ladder to the roof.

Above was the clear night sky. As soon as she stepped onto the tarred, graveled roof, Andrea was able to identify all eighty-eight of the visible constellations. Without using the binoculars, she knew on which planet opposition from the Sun would be the strongest.

Looking just above the horizon, she saw a faint light that glowed brighter than the others. To most it was just another star among thousands, to the trained eye it was Jupiter reflecting light back toward the Earth. However, to Andrea it was something more. To her it was not a distant light, or an uninhabitable planet, it was the central location of over sixty moons, one in which Andrea attempted to view from her attic while waiting for her now dead brother to return home years ago.

Sitting on the gravel, Andrea stared up at the planet, imagining the distant Callisto circling the heavens with no awareness of the planet she was sitting on, listening to the city around her come to life as people felt safe to leave the shops and homes below.

The horizon transformed from deep black to shades of purple and orange.

✳ ✳ ✳

"Andrea!"

Andrea Remus did not hear her name or feel pain from the open wound on her wrists as blood spilled to the white tiled floor. Instead she felt warm winter sunlight enter through red lace curtains from another memory of her past. The sound of a waking downtown entered with a breeze from a poorly sealed window. The bare back of Dr. Jonathan Loki pressed against her chest.

Awake, feeling the steady rhythm of Jonathan's body against her own, Andrea expected a rush of comfort throughout her body at any moment, but none came. She thought of nothing, only the unavoidable truth. In thirty minutes, she would be alone in her apartment as he dressed and returned to his wife and two daughters, bringing on feelings of dread and anxiety.

She stared at the stacks of mathematics and astrology textbooks alongside ancient works of Ovid and Theocritus beneath walls of peeling paint and a refrigerator full of nothing but dead air. Through red tint and pulled curtains she could see a closet with no new clothing, a small bathroom, and a kitchen five feet from her where she lay.

This was her life.

Andrea rose from the futon and walked to her closet. She began to dress.

Waking, Jonathan opened his eyes as Andrea put on her shoes. "What time is it?"

She focused on tying the laces. "Seven." She walked toward the door, keys in hand.

"Where are you going?"

"Close the door when you leave. Have a happy Thanksgiving."

Andrea walked out the door, leaving Jonathan Loki alone and confused as sunlight entered through red lace curtains.

✳ ✳ ✳

Thomas ran to Andrea's side as Pandora resurrected thoughts of a visit to her elementary school, following the conclusion of college graduation two decades in the past.

The rental truck, filled with a few possessions collected over four years of undergraduate study, came to a stop. Andrea put the truck in park and shut off the engine.

She opened the door, stepped out onto gravel, closed the door, and began walking toward softball fields in the distance. Wind whistled past, tangling her hair as she walked, ominous black Clouds in a late August sky above. The wind was cold, bitter, but filled with an electric charge that raised hairs along her forearm.

Stepping along beaten paths littered with withered leaves through a wooded area around the school playground, Andrea noticed branches were losing their foliage. It was silent—no bird or insect sounds. All she heard was her footfall as she approached a clearing.

In the center of a patch of dry earth and dead grass was a single tree, larger than the others. In its branches, tattered and nearly derelict, was a tree house. Feelings of comfort and security washed through Andrea's body at the sight of the weathered wood and rusted nails in the bare branches of the aged oak.

The single most pleasant object, the source of the fondest memories from her childhood, was intact. However, dead limbs had replaced the live branches.

Footsteps echoed throughout hollow woods and decomposing roots as Andrea approached her childhood haven.

Placing her foot on the first of the planks nailed to the trunk to form a ladder caused the board to split, drop, and fall to the ground. Andrea studied the rotted wood. Its insides were black and hollow.

Andrea continued to climb.

Pulling herself inside, her eyes moved from one side to the other, studying what used to be more of a home than her own room, which was permeated by fear and discomfort.

Andrea's mind retraced the location of each item she used to own. She remembered books of calculations and notes of sky watching filling the wall to the right. To the left were stacks of astronomy and science magazines with more note-books of calculations. Behind were books of mythology. And in front was the missing wall and open air, where she set up her telescope to always point at the night sky.

This was her place of comfort, her only means of surviving years of abuse and fear. Now all that remained was a collection of broken twigs, leaves, debris, and stray pages from the days before she moved away to college.

Below her fingertips, ingrained in the brown boards, were two faded circles of red. Andrea's eyes flared as she shifted her gaze from the floor to the scars on both wrists.

She went numb, her comfort evaporating. Silently looking away, she began to descend from the confines of the three walls. It was time to move on.

Standing still on the outskirts of the bordering trees, viewing the house one final time, Andrea could see small sparks of electricity move throughout the Cloud above.

Andrea whispered her last goodbyes, knowing she'd never return. She made her way back to the truck to continue her trip west to her new home and university—graduate school.

From the parking lot, Andrea looked across the street. Her mother's car sat in the driveway. Daryl was not there, but he wasn't far away. He never was.

Climbing into the truck, she put the key into the ignition. The engine would not start.

It was too late. The storm would have to pass.

Andrea sat without speaking, looking at the jet black sky, watching lighting flash from sky to ground as Thomas Charon attempted to pull her mind from the past.

"Andrea, what did you do?"

She said nothing. Her eyes were fixed, unblinking. He placed his hand to her head, too afraid to touch her wrists. Panicked, he ran to her closet, stepping through shattered glass from the broken mirror, and removed a towel. Returning, he put pressure on the wounds and continued to speak. "Anne, tell me where you are. Talk to me."

Her eyes were glazed and transfixed on the wall when, without warning, she began to fight. Kicking and flailing her arms, she hit him in the face, ripping the towel from her wrists. Thomas tried his best to control her. "Andrea, it's Tom. It's Tommy—stop!"

"I don't care! I don't care!" was all she said.

She continued to fight. It took all his strength to wrap his hands, arms, and legs around her body to keep her constrained.

Both flat on the floor now, Andrea was on top of Thomas, fighting with amazing strength as he tried to bring her back to the present. Slowly, Andrea began to grow weak as tears streamed down her face. He could hear her exhale slowly, feeling her warm tears on his face and lips, tasting the salt.

For five minutes they held one another—Thomas silent, in the present, and Andrea lost in the past—until, all at once, Andrea stopped crying, and the room went silent.

"Andrea?"

"What happened?"

Thomas loosened his grip. Andrea slid to the floor. Two drops of blood fell from her nose. "Tom, why are my wrists bleeding?"

Thomas said nothing. Instead he picked up the towel and pressed it to her wrists. As he added pressure, she began to cry. There was nothing he could say or do but hold her.

After a while he led her to the kitchen sink and turned on the water. Removing the towel, he let the water wash away the blood. Andrea cringed in pain. He let the water run until the daily allotment had been used.

Thomas reached beneath the sink and grabbed the first aid kit. Wiping away water and blood, he wrapped both wrists in gauze, then took her to the table. He sat her down and took the chair at the opposite end of the table.

Andrea stopped crying. Pain radiated throughout her head and wrists.

Neither spoke, and silence filled the room. Both feared there'd be a replay at any moment.

"What happened, Andrea? Where did you go?"

Andrea sat with her hand on the table, staring at the blood beginning to seep through the bandage.

"It's different than before, isn't it?" Andrea asked.

He sat quietly, not knowing what do. Andrea continued to stare at her wrist.

"I was coming to tell you—"

"I thought it was a fluke. I didn't say anything because I thought I could handle it. But this isn't like it was twelve years ago. It's worse. It's like the system is picking up where it left off, even though we finished our assignment to Gliese. What's going on?" She looked up from her wounds at Thomas.

"I need to show you something."

※ ※ ※

Thomas went out into the hall. Andrea followed.

Stepping into Pandora's control room, Thomas went to his work station. After typing a few words, the screen on the left went black. An access code appeared, then the screen filled with three columns of information.

The first was a column of names, the second a list of exoplanets, and in the third the word "FAILED" in capital letters.

Andrea stared. Blood began to soak through the gauze wrapped around her wrists as her pulse quickened. She stepped forward. "What's this?"

Andrea scanned the list of names. "Is that Herschel? He and his wife died a few years ago in a car crash, right? I remember reading about it in the news . . . Rosse? Wollaston? Cannon? All of them were part of the project?"

Thomas stood behind her in silence.

"Why is the word 'failed' by each couple's name?" she asked.

"It's not beside all of them."

Thomas scrolled to the bottom of the list. The name "Charon," the planet "Gliese," and the word "success" were in capital letters.

"We were the first, Anne, but not the last."

Andrea stared at the monitor as electricity filled the room. "You think they died working on Pandora?"

Thomas said nothing.

"That's ridiculous." She laughed uncomfortably as she turned toward Thomas. He didn't smile. "I'm sorry to disappoint you, but there's a flaw in your theory," she said.

"What's that?"

"It takes two to operate Pandora," she said. "Some of the people on that list didn't have partners with an understanding of astronomy, or advanced mathematics."

"So?"

"So. They wouldn't have been able to calculate the movements through the IPS using LaGrange calculations, or load memories into Pandora without a superior understanding of the advanced computer software. There has to be two. It's the one rule that cannot be broken. It's what made us special."

"But what if it was never a rule?" Thomas said. "What if all of this is one big charade?"

"What are you talking about?" Andrea was no longer laughing.

"What if we were never needed to load memories into Pandora, or chart movements through the IPS? What if all we're here for, what if everyone was chosen for—"

"For what?"

"—for their memories?"

Andrea began shaking her head, not wanting to hear what Thomas had to say. She walked toward the door. "That's ridiculous. I'm going to the research room to—"

"Think about it, Andrea. Do you really believe they'd leave our survival to human error? Especially when it comes to mapping the IPS?" He blocked the door, keeping her from leaving. She tried to move past him, but he wouldn't budge.

"We never had control. Pandora has been doing all the calculations and memory loading from day one. We were only told we were needed for calculations to make sure we participated in the project."

Andrea attempted to open the door, but he continued to block the exit. "They wanted the best minds."

"Tom. Stop."

"They wanted to make sure the memories that survived were supplied not only from the most intelligent—"

"I don't want to hear this."

"—but also from couples. They wanted to make sure partnership, love, devotion—all of it—was remembered."

"I'm serious, Tom. I don't want to hear any more. Let me out."

They continued to struggle with the door.

"The only problem was, the couples they chose were not strong enough . . .

"Shut up."

"They did not share in the other's memories . . ."

"I said, shut up." She stopped fighting with the door and put her hands over her ears.

"They experienced the flashes on their own, so weren't unable to bring themselves back. They lost their minds to Pandora, and the only reason we survived is because of the memory we shared. The emotions. We saved each other, Andrea. We beat it."

"I said shut *up!*"

Under the impact of Andrea's words, Thomas fell to the floor.

❊ ❊ ❊

"Tommy, wake up!"

Thomas looked into Andrea's red eyes as blood ran from his nose. Pain shot through his head as he tried to move.

"Tommy? Tommy, are you awake?"

Andrea's hands moved across his body, stopping at his chest before moving to his head. Her hands shook. "Don't move—just lie still." There was tension and panic in her voice.

Thomas dabbed at the blood running from his nose with his fingers as his brain throbbed in pain. Nevertheless, he sat up, blood smeared above his lip.

"Tom, we have to go. We can't stay here any longer. I'm going to open the hatch. I'll—"

"You left. Why?"

She looked at him, confused. "What are you talking about? I didn't go anywhere. I've been right here waiting for you to regain consciousness."

She softened her tone. "Do you know when you are? You may be confused—"

"I know when *and* where I am, Andrea. What I need to know is why you left."

Thomas stood and wiped the blood from his face with his sleeve. Andrea continued to kneel on the floor, looking up at him with the same lost expression.

"Tom, I think you're confused," Andrea said slowly, carefully articulating each syllable. "You fell—"

"Answer the damn question, Andrea!" His voice was abrupt and sharp, and she jumped back in surprise, her nerves raw. "Better yet, how did you hurt your wrists?"

He began to pace from one side of the room to the other, keeping his eyes locked on Andrea.

"You know how I hurt my wrists. You were—" Andrea said softly before he cut her off.

"I'm not talking about now. I'm talking about before. In the past. When you first gave yourself those scars—not when you reopened them a few moments ago."

Her eyes moved from Thomas to the floor. "I don't want to talk about that," she said.

"Of course you don't. So tell me this instead. Where did you go when you had your memory replay that forced you to cut your wrists?"

"Tom, I—"

"Or how about why you love to read mythology, your obsession with caramel milk, or maybe what happened to you at home before going to college? Hell, what happened while in college? I didn't meet you until grad school."

"Tom, I—"

"How did your brother die?"

"Tom, shut *up*!"

Andrea stood up and walked toward the door. Thomas wouldn't let her pass. "You never want to talk about it." His face was angry. There was still blood on his face.

"Tom, *move*!"

"In the few years we were married, you never wanted to talk about yourself. You never wanted me to know anything about your past. Why is that? What happened to you?" He was directly in front of her, trying to make eye contact and get answers.

Andrea's eyes remained focused on his bloodstained chest. "Tom, I told you when we first started dating—my past is my own, and if you asked questions it would be over."

"It's a good thing we're divorced then."

Andrea looked up into his eyes. For a moment, neither spoke. Then, "I'm done talking. Move."

"No."

They stood immobile, neither breaking eye contact.

"Why did you leave?"

"Why do keep asking that? What are you talking about?"

"The first day we met Munin, why did you leave?"

Andrea paused, remembering the events of that day. "Because . . . I was upset."

"Not good enough. Not this time."

Andrea stepped back and looked at him. The expression on her face changed—his remained the same.

"Not good enough? What is this really about, Tom? My refusal to tell you about my past, or your that you feel unable to save me?" Andrea was on the defense.

"This has nothing to do with me. This is about you and your past, not mine. This is about your inability to communicate with me on even the smallest issues, let alone the big ones. You never let me in. I used to believe that if I gave you enough time—"

"I would come around. That I would realize you were my knight in shining armor who I could confess all of my secrets to and feel safe in your arms for all time. That with you I could feel normal. That you would succeed with me where you failed Melissa."

Thomas stopped, not knowing what to say or how to react. They looked at one another, staring into each other's eyes. Then Thomas turned, opened the door, and walked to his room without saying another word.

"Oh, I see," Andrea called after him. "You don't want to talk when it's about you."

He opened his door.

"Tom. Wait."

With his hand still on the handle of the door, he stopped. She heaved a sigh before continuing. "Let's be serious for a moment. Let's put aside all the problems, everything dealing with our past, and focus on the facts. The facts are that in less than one hour you and I both came close to dying, and would have if we didn't have each other to pull us back to the present. I suggest we open the hatch and—"

"We can't leave," he said, turning to look at her. His face was expressionless and hard. "Before leaving, Munin placed a security mechanism on the door, preventing it from open-ing until Pandora shuts itself down for good."

They looked at each other, then Andrea turned and began walking toward the ladder to the locked hatch. Thomas re-mained still, silent. After reaching the top of the ladder, she entered a five-digit code and waited. Nothing happened. En-tering the code a second time without hearing the tumblers move, she began pushing the cover with her palm. Thomas stood quietly in the doorway of his room, looking away.

Andrea jumped from the ladder to the ground and walked back to Thomas. "Why won't it open?" Tears of anger glazed her eyes.

Turning his back, Thomas slowly walked to his bed and sat on the edge. Andrea followed but did not sit. "I knew before coming back."

"Knew what?"

"All about Pandora. What it was, how we had been lied to, and what had happened to all the others who volunteered for this same assignment."

"So you knew. You knew and you still came? More im-portantly, you knew and you didn't tell me?"

"We made an agreement."

"That agreement was broken the moment Munin lied to us."

"Andrea, listen—"

"Why didn't you tell me? Didn't you think I had a choice? Didn't you think I had a life?"

"No, Andrea. I didn't." She looked at him, shocked by his bluntness. "You haven't had a choice, *or* a life in years. To be honest, I'm not sure you know what living is."

Andrea stood silent and still, eyes moist.

"But you know what, Andrea? It's too late for that now. Neither of us had a choice. Whether you want to believe it or not, our lives are over. Not just yours and mine, but everyone's. You know it just as well as I do. Outside these walls, this world is ripping itself apart and people are dying. People with families, loved ones, people they want to spend their last remaining days with. But this is something you and I don't have. The people we loved are gone, and the only thing we have left of them are memories. It's because of this we don't have a choice. It's all our lives are good for, now. All we have left is each other, and the past."

Thomas spoke in a calm, collected, monotone voice, but Andrea heard nothing. She was no longer there. The computer of Pandora resurrected pieces and selections of her memory, sending her mind into a collage of random thoughts from her past, flowing seamlessly from one to the other before being stored into its data banks.

Remus

IN THE BEGINNING, THERE WAS DARKNESS.
White walls, tile floors, Thomas Charon, feelings, emotions—all faded. All that remained were Andrea's thoughts, flowing from one to the other, randomly, throughout the course of a lifetime, from the recesses of her mind to the files of Pandora.

Solidity took shape.

Lights appeared overhead.

✳ ✳ ✳

Students stood from darkened observatory seats and stepped toward exits, the afternoon sun and weekend freedom ahead. Professor Loki and Andrea stood in the center of the circular room as the last of her classmates left, leaving silence behind.

Andrea's bag, filled with tales of Aeneas, star maps of the Southern Hemisphere, and astrological textbooks, hung from her left shoulder. She gripped a stapled test, with A;pl in red ink on top, between her fingers.

Jonathan Loki smiled. "What can I do for you, Miss Remus?"

Andrea's face remained hard and expressionless. She held out the paper, and Jonathan stared at the grade. His smile remained.

"I'm not sure how I can improve a perfect score, but I'm open to suggestions."

Not amused, Andrea flipped to page two, which contained a complete list of all known moons orbiting Jupiter. She pointed to question thirty-four.

Studying the page, Jonathan quickly realized the mistake.

"That's not supposed to be there. Dido orbits Saturn, not Jupiter," said the girl.

Jonathan pondered possible solutions. "Well, Miss Re-mus—t seems I made a mistake grading your test. Dido isn't the correct answer for number thirty-four, but I guess you already knew that."

Andrea remained silent. Professor Loki continued to smile. "But I'll make a deal with you. Rather than go through the hassle of changing grades and subtracting points, when you clearly know the answer is Io, let's leave it. We'll call it a gift for being honest. But that's only if you promise not to tell any of the other students. I don't want to hear them complain, think I have favorites. You know how they are."

Andrea looked into Loki's eyes, startled. "What did you say?"

He held his smile. "That I won't tell if you won't. It'll be our little secret. But if you believe the three points you earned illegally constitutes an ethical breach of contract, I can lower the grade and remove the points." He chuckled and handed the test back to her. "I'm not as evil as my name implies."

She didn't take the pages. Instead she studied the face of the man before her, as if he were a ghostly reincarnation of an ancient memory stating the words of Michael Balder Remus with the strange voice of a middle-aged professor of college astronomy.

Without explanation, and with a sad expression, Andrea let her bag slip from her shoulder to the floor and took a slow step toward Professor Loki.

Test still in hand, Jonathan took a half step back, Andrea's body now inches away.

They looked at one another. He wore a bewildered expression. Hers remained the same.

Andrea rested her hand on the professor's waist, lifted herself to her tiptoes—and pressed her mouth to his.

Jonathan hesitated, pulling his head back as far possible, before giving in. Her eyes closed as his remained open.

Andrea probed his mouth with her tongue. Loki's hands remained pinned to his side as his eyes closed, his tongue reciprocating as they exchanged mixed emotions.

As her temporary lapse of logical conscientiousness ended, Andrea's eyes opened and her lips separated from his. Removing her hands from his waist, she took a single step back, still focused on his face.

She saw a shocked expression.

Her expression remained the same—emotionless, sad eyes that realized nothing had changed. No new feelings emerged to erase memories of a morbid past, setting everything right, and resurrecting stagnant personalities. Andrea remained the same.

She lifted her bag from the ground and walked toward the exit.

Confused, Professor Jonathan Loki said nothing.

Sunlight filled the room as Andrea opened the observatory's double doors and walked from the future to the past through the suburban middle-school doors of her childhood toward buses alongside the building, clothes wrinkled and eyes focused on the pavement.

Children running toward their assigned buses were chattering and laughing. The ambient noise of parents and colors of minivans faded into the background as Andrea, exhausted from lack of sleep while watching the night sky, wandered in and out of consciousness. The whine of distant sirens pulled her to reality.

Movement ceased. Smiles faded. Excitement evaporated.

All looked to the sky. Buses, cars, and SUVs cut their engines as everyone hurried toward the school entrance.

Andrea remained still.

Sirens grew louder with each passing moment as parents, students, and drivers shuffled toward the school. They all avoided Andrea. As the last of them passed through the doors of the school, the Sirens faded. Only muffled silence and Andrea remained.

Lifting her head, she walked along the pavement, turned left, and continued down the abandoned road. Sunlight shined from a clear sky, revealing no sign of the approaching threat.

Sweat speckled her brow. The afternoon air remained stifling and stagnant.

With each step away from the desks and students, her hollow footsteps echoed off vacant playgrounds littered with motionless kickballs, empty chalk outlines of four square, and drooping basketball nets mounted on white backboards.

Stunted shrubs lined the empty sidewalks. Trees and branches absent of life stood motionless. Streets were filled with empty vehicles in every lane, doors closed and locked, ignitions off.

Windows were dark, homes empty, each filled with invisible families and strangers. All were afraid. Silence and stillness filled the air as the temperature dropped dramatically. The hair on Andrea's forearm stood on end.

Shivering, she stepped through the door of her empty home. Windows were coated with frost as she walked upstairs to her room and closed the door. As she lay on the bed, she stared at the outline of the approaching black figure. White light illuminated barren ground through clear panes, penetrating through hardened soil. The sill of her window froze shut, allowing thoughts to transfer from the security of her room with neon stars pasted on the ceiling, to sheets of ice through closed car windows as they melted from the roofs, crashing to the ground outside the motionless vehicle.

Tales of the House of Atreus rested on her lap, closed.

Evelyn Remus sat in the driver's seat of her car, staring straight ahead. Each house in the neighborhood, frozen limb on partially dead trees, and frosted white lawns surrounding their home were motionless and silent.

"You can't keep doing this, Andrea. Do you see what could happen if you stay out during an Outage? Look at the neighborhood. Because the weather changes so dramatically because of the Clouds you could get hypothermia, heat exhaustion, or worse. You know this better than anyone after what happened to Michael. What are you trying to prove?"

Evelyn turned to Andrea sitting in the passenger seat of the car, who kept her eyes on the thawing ice falling from the roofs and trees along the street. "Where do you go?"

No reply.

"Why won't you talk to me? I know I shouldn't leave you alone at night, but I have to work. Without Michael's help, I don't know what we're going to do now. We were barely making it before."

Moments passed with still no reply. Evelyn kept her eyes on Andrea. "What happened, Andrea? What happened that night?"

Andrea did not stir. Evelyn heaved a heavy sigh and reached for Andrea's hand, then withdrew. She started the car and shifted into drive, but kept her foot on the brake. "I'm marrying Daryl."

Andrea turned from the window to the face of her mother.

Evelyn did not look at her daughter, instead keeping her eyes on the front windshield. "He's moving in next week. He's going to watch you while I'm at work. Luckily he was able to pull some strings and switch supervisor shifts with someone else."

Evelyn Remus moved her foot from the brake to the accelerator, then pulled out onto the street. "Everything's going to be fine. Trust me," she said as she drove.

Andrea's hands began to shake as she turned the page past the tale of Iphigemia. Her nerves steadied as thoughts, images, and speech reversed in age, settling on myths of the creation she first read with her brother years ago, when he was alive.

Michael Remus sat on the sofa in the attic beside his younger sister. Her eyes glued to the page. "What're you reading?"

"Mythology."

"Again? How many times are you going to read that book? I would have never told you that story about Romulus and Remus if I knew you were going to become obsessed."

"I'm not obsessed."

"Really? When you're not reading that old book of mythology, your nose is glued to a book or magazine about astronomy. That's obsessed, my dear little sister."

"This is different. After what you told me about gods and where we came from, I wanted to know why the planets were named after Roman gods, so I found this at the library."

"*Mythology* by Edith Hamilton," Michael read aloud.

"Did you know the Romans believed the universe was ruled by huge monsters they called Titans?"

"Really?" Michael, feigning ignorance, took the book from Andrea's hands and flipped through the pages and illustrations.

"Yeah. They looked like us, but they were huge, evil, and ugly. They thought the world, before they came here, was completely crazy and dangerous. They thought it was controlled by hurricanes, tornadoes, volcanoes, and other bad stuff."

"Sounds familiar."

Andrea stared at Thomas, confused. "No it doesn't."

"It doesn't? Think about it, Midget. With all these Clouds, lightning, and power Outages, it sounds more like ancient mythology rather than reality. Know what I mean?"

Andrea thought for a moment before answering. "I didn't think of that."

Michael handed the book back to Andrea. "So, tell me, Professor Remus, how did everything get put into proper working order?" he asked jokingly.

"Well, Jupiter, the king of the gods, with his four brothers and sisters, fought the Titans in a huge war. When it was all over, the gods had won. To fix the problems of the world, and make it not so crazy, they locked each Titan in a pit deep within the earth near the underworld, Tartarus. See?"

Andrea opened the book to a picture of all the ancient monsters behind their prison. Jupiter looked down from on high.

"What would happen if the Titans got out?"

"I . . . I don't know." She giggled. "But it's not true. It's just myth, Mike."

Michael smiled. "I know. But all myths have to start somewhere. They all have an origin. Remember what I told you about where we came from?"

A breeze blew through the open window, causing the old telescope to sway. The form of Michael vanished from her thoughts as the white light of distant stars appeared.

Andrea's teenage hand steadied the telescope as she looked through the eyepiece at the clear night sky.

The attic steps creaked beneath Daryl Tyr's feet as he peered through the railing at Andrea's . He watched in silence. The steps moaned as he shifted his weight.

Startled, Andrea looked toward the stairs.

Daryl stared through the darkness with a menacing smile. He climbed the last steps, turned the corner, and walked toward Andrea. Neither took their eyes off the other.

"Evelyn told me you loved astronomy, but she didn't tell me about all this. You have your own personal observatory up here." His voice was filled with mock enthusiasm. Magazines, journals, and notes were in stacks across the floor and around the couch.

"She said you spend most of your time up here studying mythology, reading magazines, and taking notes. Very intelligent for a girl your age, but I guess it helps occupy your time, now that your brother's gone."

Andrea glared at him.

Daryl continued to smile. On the sofa a book of mythology lay open, face down. "What story are you reading?"

Andrea kept her eyes on Daryl without speaking.

"Evelyn also told me you weren't much of a talker. But what she didn't mention was how pretty you are. But I guess that goes without saying."

The sound of moving tree limbs, half frozen from the previous Outage, absent of foliage and life, filled the room.

Suddenly, Daryl looked as if he had been struck by lightning. "I'm sorry. How rude of me. We haven't been formally introduced. I'm Daryl. I work with your mom at the plant as the third shift supervisor."

Daryl Tyr held out his hand.

Andrea went back to studying the night sky.

Daryl continued to speak. "You may have noticed me at the funeral. I was sitting next to your mother. I meant to introduce myself, but you vanished before I had a chance."

Andrea continued to look through the telescope, paying no attention to the man.

Daryl placed his fingers on the back of Andrea's neck. "Mind if I take a look."

Andrea quickly moved her head and stepped away. His smile remained. Looking through the eyepiece Daryl lifted his head and looked to Andrea. "It's Jupiter, right?"

Andrea said nothing. Daryl continued to smile, moving hands from his sides to his pockets. Both stood, staring at the other. "Your mother just wanted me to come up, introduce myself, and tell you dinner was ready."

Daryl turned and walked toward the stairs.

"It was nice to meet you, Andrea. We'll talk more later. I have a feeling we'll be seeing a lot more of each other." Daryl did not look back.

Andrea stood in silence as the wind continued to blow in the darkness. She closed her eyes, focusing on the silence of the attic and the memory of her brother before opening her eyes to the sound of Michael's voice and face hovering over her own. "Andrea, wake up."

Andrea's eyes fluttered open. The room was dark. "What is it?"

"Get dressed."

"Is it time for you to leave already?"

"No. Not yet. I have something to show you. Get your jacket—it's still cold outside."

Grabbing her jacket and shoes, Andrea followed Michael down the stairs to the front door. She waited until she reached safety outside, with the door securely shut, before putting on sneakers.

"Where are we going?" Andrea forced her foot inside the laced shoe.

"To the trails behind the school. It's not that far. We should be back before Mom wakes up. Ready?"

Yawning, Andrea shook her head.

"Let's go."

Following Michael's footsteps, the two made their way across the lawn toward the elementary school playground.

Andrea and Michael crossed into the forest. The sun had begun to peek over the horizon to warm the day and push away the night. Trees and grass were tinted blue.

Walking into the woods, Andrea did not ask questions. She followed Michael with trust and curiosity.

Turning down certain paths, moving deeper into the woods, Michael made his way off the beaten track and continued walking forward, deep into the trees and bushes.

Stepping over fallen branches and through piles of leaves, Michael and Andrea made their way toward a clearing. A single tree stood in its center, isolated from the others. In its branches was a tree house built of wood.

"Wow!" Andrea looked up in amazement, now fully awake.

Michael smiled.

He made his way to a twill rope dangling from a hole cut in the mismatched wooden floorboards. Planks were nailed into the trunk as a ladder leading up into the tree house. Andrea looked at the structure in amazement.

"Did you build this?"

Michael chuckled. "No—I found it when I was about your age. But I did knock out one of the walls. Come on—I'll show you."

Michael began climbing, with Andrea right behind.

The six planks led to an opening cut in the floorboards. Inside were three walls, a ceiling, and the trunk of the tree in its center. The north wall was gone, with only a thin wooden slat nailed across its center. Andrea looked out at the cloudy morning sky.

"I figured you could stay here while I'm gone. Not permanently, but anytime you need to get out of the house, you can come out here and look at the stars instead of being stuck in the attic, waiting for me to come home. I didn't tell Mom about it, so this place is completely yours."

Andrea wrapped her arms around Michael's neck, tackling him to the floor. He screamed and laughed. "Thank you! Thank you! Thank you!"

"You're welcome Midget."

Andrea hugged her brother close. "I'm going to miss you Mike."

"I'm going to miss you too."

Andrea squeezed and held as tight as she could to her brother's body, not wanting to let go—only to find herself gripping the bare back of Professor Jonathan Loki years in the future. She wanted to scream.

Exhausted and out of breath, Jonathan fell to the opposite side of the futon beside her. Breathing heavily, looking at the ceiling, Andrea turned on her side, her back to him. She curled into the fetal position and lay there naked, legs pulled to her stomach and chest.

Getting up, Jonathan dressed and walked out the door. They hadn't exchanged a single word since he'd arrived. Andrea lay on the futon in her apartment, exposed and hollow, wishing for the loneliness to dissipate. Darkness fell as her thoughts continued forward, mingling past and future memories as light danced across her studio apartment on a separate night in the past.

Jonathan lay face down, naked, asleep on the thin mattress beside her.

Images of swirling compasses, spinning in all directions without explanation, navigational equipment roaming out of control, birds flying directly into the engines of planes, and numerous beached whales, in areas all across the globe, appeared on the newly bought, used television screen in her apartment.

A reporter moved from person to person, asking each for their thoughts. Andrea could not understand what they were saying, but she could see the fear in their eyes on the television opposite her in her childhood home as Pandora transitioned seamlessly from one memory to the next before she continued to read a book of backyard astronomy by the lamplight of her living room as each item in her studio apartment dissolved and faded.

Andrea sat cross legged, staring at pictures of far-reaching galaxies she could not see through her telescope in the attic.

Michael sat contently, watching the seven o'clock news. He turned up the volume. ". . . and scientists remain baffled, unable to explain the disappearance of Florida's pelicans."

Andrea turned her attention from the book to the screen.

"The brown pelican, recently taken off the endangered species list, has been placed back on. Pelicans throughout Florida either have been found dead along sides of highways, dying as they wash up on shores, or are simply gone. Scientists are performing blood work to determine the cause of this recent occurrence, but so far no explanations have been found."

Andrea turned her attention back to her book. Beyond the borders of her page, the living room couches shifted and her brother was replaced by Daryl's image as he sat beside her still body and staring at the television, motionless and silent, as the news report continued.

"A dramatic drop in bee populations has occurred all across the country. From what scientists and beekeepers have been able to gather, the insects have disappeared, not died. Experts such as Dr. George Abell, here beside me, visited the hives to find them empty. The bees have simply vanished, without cause or explanation.

"Many scientists theorize that without bees to assist in the pollination of crops, the planet would be unable to support human life in a matter of years. Even Albert Einstein is believed to have held this view. Of course, this is a theory, but no one knows where the bees have gone."

Andrea did not shift her attention from the January Northern Latitudes sky map.

Daryl sat quietly, one arm draped over Evelyn's sleeping form, the other on his lap. When a commercial appeared, Daryl brought his hand from his lap to Andrea's knee.

Andrea took her eyes from the page to Daryl's hand. She stared, but did not move.

Daryl continued to stare at the screen.

Andrea tried to move her leg away, but Daryl gripped her thigh just above her knee, squeezing her flesh with the tips of his fingers.

Andrea winced in pain, but she did not move.

Daryl continued to watch television, loosening his grip but not removing his hand. Unsure of how to react, Andrea sat still, attempting to focus on the image of the orange and purple nebula on the page.

Daryl slowly began moving his hand from Andrea's knee to her inner thigh.

Andrea sat, paralyzed by fear.

His eyes remained on the screen.

Evelyn continued to sleep.

Daryl's hand continued to move along Andrea's thigh toward her pelvis. Fear spread as she attempted to move. Daryl gripped her thigh, harder than before. Tears welled in her eyes. He did not stop, even though his eyes remained on the screen.

Andrea continued to struggle, but Daryl's grip tightened.

Tears fell from Andrea's eyes, but she continued to wrestle her leg away. Her movements jostled the couch, causing Evelyn to stir. Daryl loosened his grip. Andrea stood. Daryl returned his hand to his lap.

Wiping tears from her eyes, Andrea turned to Daryl. Evelyn remained asleep. Daryl looked from the screen to Andrea as a smile spread across his face. There was a noticeable bulge in his jeans.

Silent and afraid, Andrea walked to the front door, tears streaming from her eyes. Book still in hand, she walked out the door of her childhood home and into the hall of her studio apartment years in the future, the book vanishing from her fingers as the years advanced. Ensuring the door was locked, then placing the single key above the frame of the door, she walked down the smoke-scented stairs onto the main street. She turned right toward the approaching blackness, and the college campus.

She began to run.

No sounds came from surrounding vehicles. Her thoughts were as quiet as her surroundings, her footsteps echoing off the filled buildings and vacant cars. She approached the campus as the large Cloud hovered above.

The weather remained constant. The temperature did not fluctuate.

Andrea's breath came out in exhausted heaves as sweat dripped from her face to the shirt plastered to her body. Her arms pumped as she ran past empty beer cans and Greek-lettered houses. Her legs pushed ever forward toward the blackness ahead and above.

With each step toward the campus, the Cloud retreated. Andrea quickened her pace. It did the same. Sunlight began to return.

Legs burning, feet heavy as lead, she ran past crowded dorms, classrooms of silent students, bike racks, empty quads, and a lonely school crest. Andrea, on the heels of the fleeing Cloud, stretched desperately to reach its boundaries. She ran past the parking lot and away from the football field before stopping at the chain-link fence separating the outskirts of the campus from the highway.

Hands on her hips, eyes to the sky, Andrea watched as the black abyss withdrew, as if being pulled by a rope.

Exhausted, Andrea grasped the fence with both hands as she struggled for air, trying to relieve the pain in her lungs. She stood and stared as her exhaustion subsided.

Vehicles along side the highway started their engines and traffic began to flow. Traffic lights functioned again. People left the safety of their dorms and classrooms. Andrea turned from the dilapidated fence, sweat dripping from her face, years peeling away as her shortening legs took her toward the woods and to the tree house left to her by her brother. With the last load of books, magazines, and equipment from the attic, she pulled the rusted wagon through the abandoned softball field as sunlight began to fade.

Stopping below the tree house, Andrea unloaded the wagon on the dry ground directly under the opening in the floorboards. Taking one handful at a time, she transported each book and scientific magazine to the confines of the tree.

By the time she'd finished, the sun had completely set. The forest was cold and quiet. Few insects and animals could be heard. Stars winked down from a clear sky.

Exhausted, yet at ease, Andrea began to methodically assemble and orient the telescope. When she was finished, she put her eye to the eyepiece and found the constellations of Aquila, Lyra, and Cygnus. Her eyes remained on the sky for hours before she was overcome by fatigue. Her eyes closed as she continued to stand at the telescope.

Exhausted, Andrea retreated to a corner of her small house, the telescope in the corner fading. She picked up an astronomy magazine resting on the floorboards just as the wooden planks dissolved beneath her feet. Her eyes, growing older with each passing moment, scanned the page of the magazine as scientific explanations were replaced by the handwritten words of Professor Jonathan Loki.

Andrea,

Let me be the first to congratulate you on being accepted into graduate school. I called in a favor to ensure your placement in the astronomy program. You will receive the letter of notification in the next few weeks.

Please don't think I made the call for personal reasons, or that's why you were accepted. You have excellent grades, and a better understanding of cosmic movements than most PhDs. I called because competition to get into graduate school has become fierce over the years because of the increase in Clouds, and people are looking to the sky for answers.

I know you will be leaving soon, and graduation is only about a week away, but I just wanted to be sure that I said goodbye. My wife, children, and I have decided to take a cross-country road trip, visiting national parks from one side of the country to the other. Recent reports estimate that most trees will be dead within the next five years, and we want to see them before they become completely extinct. By the time you get this, I'll already be gone. Lovell will be administering the final, but I already placed an A as your final grade for the course, regardless of the results.

I apologize for the abrupt farewell, and not attending the graduation ceremony, but I believe it's for the best. I wish you the best of luck. I wish there was more I could write, but there isn't.

Jonathan Loki

Behind the letter was her astronomy test from the previous year. The grade remained the same. Andrea folded both the letter and astronomy test, placed them in the trash, and allowed her saddened emotions to transport her thoughts to similar memories in the past.

The final words of the ceremony were spoken. Daryl Tyr lifted the veil of Evelyn Remus Tyr, placed his hand to her cheek, and kissed her lips.

The crowd applauded. The two separated and walked down the aisle hand in hand, smiling. Andrea stood still, silent, unable to make out the figures through her tears.

She blinked, replacing the image of her mother and stepfather with that of her brother.

"Don't cry, Anne—I'll be fine," he said.

"But what if you're not? What if something happens to you and you don't come back?" She continued to cry, speaking through sobs. "The Outages are happening every-where. What if you get stuck in the center of one because you're out alone in some desert?"

Michael chuckled softly. "I thought you weren't afraid of the Clouds."

"This is serious, Mike." Andrea pounded her fist to the mattress, looking away, profile facing the dark window. Tears continued to stream down her cheeks.

Michael's smile faded.

"Why do you have to go anyway?"

"You know why."

"Isn't there some other way?"

"Andrea—"

"Something bad is happening. I can't believe people can still only think of armies and fighting."

"You know that's not why I'm going."

"But you're still leaving."

Michael's voice rose. "We need *money*!"

Andrea stopped speaking as tears continued to well in her eyes. Michael's tone softened. "No one is hiring—mostly because of the Outages. So many companies are losing money, they can't afford to hire new people. The military is the only choice."

Andrea said nothing as she continued to face the win-dow, tears streaking down her cheek. Michael placed his fingers under her chin and turned her head toward him. She wouldn't meet his eyes, so he lifted her head. They looked at one another.

Michael smiled. "I need you to do something for me while I'm gone."

Andrea said nothing. Tears continued to fall.

"I need you to look after Mom for me. It's going to be hard with me gone, and she's going to need you to get through this. I've got a feeling some hard times are on the way. Do what needs to be done to make sure she's okay. Can you do that for me?"

Andrea nodded.

"Even if something should happen to me."

"Mike—"

"Andrea—I need you to promise to help Mom in any way you can. She can't do this on her own. I'm doing my part and I need you to do yours. Even if you don't want to, I need you to. Can you promise me that? Can you?"

Hesitantly, tears continuing to fall from her eyes, she responded with a tentative "yes."

She wiped her face and eyes to see the airport packed with delayed passengers and disgruntled relatives separated from their loved ones for the holiday season. Decorations lined the windows of overpriced shops.

Looking up, TVs showing the news grabbed her attention. Their audio was muted, and the terminal was filled with the murmur of restless conversations, so she read the captions below images of rainstorms, ice, snow, sudden heat waves, and tornadoes ravaging areas of the Midwest and East Coast. Maps of the regions displayed black masses as possible locations of Clouds. "Titans," Andrea whispered to herself.

Outside the terminal, snowflakes fell from the sky, blanketing everything. All departures and arrivals were marked with the word "canceled" in bold letters, except one.

"Good thing his plane got in the air when it did," Evelyn said to Andrea. They looked toward Gate 31B in anticipation.

The door opened, and a smile spread across Andrea's face as Michael Remus exited the plane first and walked toward his mother and sister. Before they could touch, Andrea found herself standing in the center of a room, silent, still, and absent of thought. The walls closed in. Suits, dresses, and morbid tones filtered through the crowd. Evelyn sat on the couch, surrounded by friends and family. Tears streamed down her face.

Andrea felt nothing.

A man Andrea didn't recognize stood beside Evelyn Remus, his arm around her. Andrea and the man made eye contact briefly before she looked away. The man did not.

Andrea did not cry over the loss of her brother, and had not cried since the night of the accident. Nothing had changed for her that tears could fix.

She made her way through the mourners to the front door and walked across the front yard, through two lanes of traffic, over the snow-covered softball field, and through the woods to the tree house in the center of the clearing. All was white, brown, and gray through bare tree branches.

Andrea climbed the planks on the trunk and sat alone in the center of the house. Surrounded by dead limbs and snow, she looked out at the gray clouded sky. She shed no tears—just expressed a silent wish for a happy New Year. Days passed as quickly as moments as she stood, turned, and walked into her mother's house wearing the same clothes from the night before. Evelyn sat at the kitchen table, past due mortgage, utilities, car loan, and credit card bills spread around her. The stranger from the funeral was there. Both stared at Andrea. She didn't make eye contact, just walked silently to the stairs.

"Andrea! Where have you been?"

Andrea stopped, but she did not speak.

"I haven't seen you in two days. I didn't know if you were sick, hurt, anything. When Daryl and I came in from work yesterday morning, the door was unlocked, the lights were out, and you were nowhere to be found. There were Clouds in the area! Do you know how worried I was? If I hadn't called the school and found out you were in class, I would have had to call the police. Do you have any idea what they would do if they knew I leave you here alone most nights? Where did you go? Have you even showered?"

She didn't turn toward her mother. The stranger said nothing, just stared. The tension was palpable as both waited for Andrea to speak. "*Say* something!" her mother yelled.

Andrea said nothing. Instead she walked through the kitchen past her mother, past the stranger and toward the stairs.

"Andrea!"

Evelyn Remus did not stand up from the kitchen table. Andrea did not stop as she walked through the living room.

"I'm *talking* to you!"

When Andrea did not return, Evelyn stood and made her way toward her daughter. Andrea's left foot had just touched the first step when Evelyn grabbed her shoulder, halting her progress, and pushed her against the wall. Andrea didn't fight; instead she looked at her mother with the same blank stare that she'd worn for months.

The man sitting at the kitchen table stood and walked into the living room. He said nothing—he just watched as Evelyn began yelling at her daughter's blank face.

"I don't know what your problem is, but it stops now! This has been going on for months, and I'm sick of it. Do you think you're the only one who misses him? Do you think you're the only one hurting? Well, you're not! I went through the same thing with your father. I think about Michael every day. I see his face everywhere I go. I can't get away from it."

Evelyn took her hand from Andrea's shoulder. She closed her eyes to calm herself before opening them and speaking in a gentler tone. "I know you're having a hard time dealing with this, and that astronomy is your way of dealing with Michael's death. You pretend as though you're not afraid of those Clouds, but you know better than any of us how dangerous they can be. You can't go out when they're around. It's not safe."

Andrea wanted to ask why, but she held her tongue.

"I just want you to talk to me. Let me help. Let me in. We can get through this together. Just say something—anything. Yell at the top of your lungs. Tell me I'm the worst mother who ever lived. Tell me you hate me, this life—anything!"

Andrea balled her fists. Evelyn noticed a piece of paper in her hand.

"What's this?" Evelyn asked, reaching for the crumpled paper. Unfolding the creases, she flattened the paper and saw a column of A's down the center of the report card.

Evelyn didn't speak—she just went to sit on the living room couch. The man looked at the paper too. Andrea took the stairs to the attic and gently closed the door. The man watched as she made her exit. Evelyn took no notice.

Andrea walked up the stairs to the attic, turned the corner, and in an instant entered the campus observatory.

"Andrea, may I speak with you a moment?" Andrea let the other students pass. "You forgot your test." Professor Loki held up the graded test with an awkward smile that quickly faded.

Andrea, backpack slung across her left shoulder, was unable to look into Loki's eyes. Neither knew what to say.

"Miss Remus, I—"

Andrea spoke before he could finish his thought. "I won't be going home for break."

Jonathan looked at her, confused. "What?"

"My address is on my contact information, but don't think about calling. I don't have a phone. If I'm not there, I'm on the roof. Just come up."

Without giving Jonathan an opportunity to stammer a response, Andrea began walking toward the double doors. "You can keep my test until then."

Walking through the room, Andrea kept her eyes on the floor. With each step, black scratches appeared as the maroon carpet transformed into white paper, and words appeared before her eyes from the book in her lap. Sirens could be heard for a moment before lights throughout the neighborhood went out.

The room went dark.

With the book of mythology still on her lap, Andrea looked out the attic window to the darkened night sky. There were no stars. She put the book on the floor beside the sofa.

Daryl Tyr stood before her. He did not move. He did not speak. In the darkness, Andrea could only see the outline of his face. Neither moved. Each looked at the other. The temperature in the room began to drop.

Reaching down, Daryl took Andrea's hands and pulled them above her head as he forced her back into the sofa cushions. His grip was firm.

Maneuvering his body on top of hers, Daryl kept her legs pinned and parted with his weight. "If you and your mom want to keep your house, you better keep quiet," he said.

Afraid, Andrea screamed, fighting as hard as she could before he knocked her unconscious with his fist.

The room went black.

Andrea awoke to pain as Daryl thrust into her. She was too weak to scream or fight back. The side of Daryl's face was pressed against her own. He continued to grip her hands.

Daryl's pace quickened as he moaned in pleasure.

Tears streamed down the side of her face. The pain became unbearable. The thought of what was taking place washed all others from her mind.

Daryl took one hand from Andrea's wrists and caressed her face, then ran it down the length of her body as he kept hold of her wrists with the other hand.

Andrea shook her head from side to side, as if trying to fling out all awareness of what was taking place. She screamed in horror.

Daryl moaned in ecstasy, and with one final, painful thrust, it was done. Neither moved.

Sighs and tears left Andrea's mouth and eyes. Daryl moved his hand across her partially exposed stomach and adolescent breasts before slowly lifting himself from her.

Andrea moaned softly as a new pain replaced the other, the feeling of sharp steel splitting her skin, causing blood to spill from her wrists to the floorboards of the tree house.

She watched in silence, feeling her pulse quicken as blood flowed from her body out her open veins. She heard the blade as it hit the floorboards.

In the distance, she could hear the sound of approaching footsteps and someone calling her name. She closed her eyes to black mist, the sound of her own screams, the impact of steel from a car out of control. Her body jerked forward with enough force to knock her unconscious as it remained trapped inside the walls of Pandora.

❋ ❋ ❋

Thomas Charon could hear whispers of apologies for broken promises from Andrea's lips as he attempted to retrieve her mind. Blood ran from her nose.

Her mind continued to move from memory to memory as he called for her to return to the present. Pain shot through his head.

In bloodstained clothing, he ran across lanes of motionless cars beneath a black sky, the memories of his past moving freely, all copied and stored to Pandora's databanks.

Charon

ALL WAS DARK, SILENT.

The air was filled with the scent of grass and bark, but shadows from overhanging branches were absent. Thomas stripped off his white shirt and let it drop to the ground. There was no rain, but white light flashed from the large black Cloud that covered the afternoon sky, making it as black as night.

The temperature began to rise.

Kicking off his black dress shoes, he continued to run across dry grass in his white socks. Sweat ran in torrents down his back and from his forehead. Exhaustion spread through his muscles. The city park remained silent as it absorbed each labored breath into its dying branches, returning each long stride as an echo.

Still running, Thomas fumbled with the zipper of his jeans. Undoing the top button, he let the blood-soaked pants slip from his thighs, and with a fluid motion, kicked them to the ground. Leaving his clothing behind, he continued to run deeper into the deserted park. Lightning, absent of thunder, flashed from above, illuminating his nearly naked body.

Maneuvering over trails, past dying trees, and across parched grass of brown and yellow, Thomas dripped sweat as the temperature continued to rise and he ran even faster.

A pair of boxers and a pair of socks were all that could be seen moving through the remaining trees and dying shrubs. Exhaustion punished his lungs and made him stagger. The image of his father on the bathroom floor was all that kept his muscles from failing.

Out of breath, he finally stopped. Gasping, he hunched over, hands on his knees, eyes to the ground. Gathering his strength, his breath became more relaxed and controlled as he stood and put his hands to his sides. He looked at the black sky. White light moved through its interior, giving the darkness shape, form, definition. Tree branches were empty and playgrounds were vacant. Shadows were all he could see.

He began to run again, leaving clothing soaked in his father's blood in the past as darkness dissolved, and sunlight shined down from a bright blue afternoon sky. Pandora progressed to another memory from his past as cars passed in a hurry, making their way home.

Thomas waited, standing at an intersection, breathing controlled, and pulse even, waiting for the approaching black Clouds overhead.

A stranger approached him from behind . Thomas kept his eyes forward on the distant sky.

"Tom?"

Behind him stood Melissa Pomene, sweat trickling from her pulled-back hair, down her neck to her sports bra and bare belly. He turned toward the road and cloudy sky.

"Tom, it's Melissa."

Thomas said nothing. He continued forward as the traffic light and cars turned.

"*Charon!*" Melissa called from the vacated intersection. Thomas did not turn back. Sirens came to life, but he kept his eyes on the road ahead, knowing the Cloud was approaching.

In the distance, lightning struck the pavement. Melissa Pomene went silent.

Cars stopped in streets. Traffic, street, and building lights extinguished. People quickly left their vehicles and walked to the safety of the nearest home or store.

Not hearing Melissa's footsteps, he stopped and turned back toward the intersection. She had not moved. She stared at the sky as the Cloud continued to approach, sending lightning to the ground.

Thomas returned to the intersection. "Melissa!"

She looked at him, eyes filled with tears and fear.

"Can you run?" he asked.

Without answering, she looked to the sky. Lightning continued to strike pavement some distance ahead. She jumped.

The Sirens went silent. The world grew quiet and dark. Only Thomas and Melissa remained on the street.

"*Mel*!"

She turned to Thomas. Tears fell from her eyes.

"Can you run?" he asked again, carefully enunciating each word to make sure she understood. She nodded.

"Follow me." He ran from the approaching Cloud, and Melissa followed.

The day grew black. The temperature increased. Thomas ran down the street of vacated cars, passing houses and businesses with closed doors and blank windows. He picked up speed, and Melissa's footsteps echoed behind his own.

Thomas turned off the main street onto Wilson Drive. Maneuvering between stranded vehicles, they made it to the front door of his home just as Laura Charon swung it open. "Get in here, you two. Hurry!" she said.

Lightning hit the lawn as they entered, shaking the ground. When the door closed, the foyer went black, erasing the memory of his mother, and Melissa. In its place he saw Charles Charon rubbing his temples and severed leg

Thomas sat in a chair beside his father's bed and stared at blood seeping through the bandages. "What's wrong?" he asked

Charles said nothing. He continued to rub his head and leg. "Dad, are you okay?" His father remained silent.

"*Dad.*"

"What!?"

Thomas paused, then said again, "Are you okay?"

"Yes! I'm fine!" Charles let his nerves settle. "I'm sorry, Tom. It's just that my head and leg hurt all of a sudden. I'm not sure why, but . . . I'll be fine."

Charles forced a smile before the lights went out. The sky went black. Thomas looked at his father, whose pain increased. "Dad?"

Charles groaned in pain. "Get the nurse."

Thomas went to the hall, where chaos reigned. Hospital attendants were going through the halls with hand-held generators.

"Excuse me?" Thomas went unnoticed. "Excuse me?"

Thomas grabbed the sleeve of a nurse, who said, "Please return to your room."

"But it's my dad—"

"Does he need a generator? Is he on life support?"

"No, but his head and leg—"

"I'm sorry, but if your father isn't on life support, he is going to have to wait until the Outage has passed."

"But—"

"I'm sorry."

The nurse walked away in a hurry. Thomas returned to his father's room. Charles lay in his bed, unsure of how to deal with the pain. He was on his back, eyes closed, wincing, attempting to massage both his leg and head at the same time.

"Dad, all the nurses are busy."

"Get . . ." The pain was too much.

"What's wrong?"

"It feels like my head is being split in half. Like my leg is still there, and someone is running over it with a truck!"

Charles screamed, and Thomas, terrified, ran to the side of the bed. "What can I do?"

"Find some aspirin, ibuprofen, codeine, anything! Something to stop the pain!"

Thomas left room 327, his father's screams in the background as his thoughts transitioned from the hospital to a chair in his basement, years earlier.

"Are you okay?" he was saying.

"Yeah, fine. Just had something stuck in my throat," said Melissa.

She gave Laura Charon a smile of reassurance before turning to look at Thomas, who sat in a chair at the side of the room, staring into space. Scented candles illuminated the basement, masking the smell of mildew with lavender.

"What happened?" Melissa said. "I haven't seen or heard from you in years. Where have you been? I came over the day you were supposed to leave, but I guessed you'd already left because no one answered the door, which I thought odd. I tried calling you at school, but I couldn't find your number.

I even wrote to the address you gave to me, but it came back 'Return to sender.' It was as if you dropped off the face of the planet. Where have you been for the last two years?"

Thomas said nothing. Sweat dripped from Melissa's face. The house radiated heat.

"He never left."

Melissa turned to Laura Charon, the smile washing from her face. "What?" Melissa looked from Thomas to Laura.

"After the funeral, Tom lost interest in college," Laura said.

"What about the scholarships?"

"He gave them back."

"But . . ." It was clear to Thomas that Melissa was confused, but she couldn't seem to find the words to articulate what puzzled her. Lightning flashed through the basement window, illuminating the dark.

Candles flickered. "Where have you been?" she asked again.

Thomas still said nothing. He would not meet her gaze.

Realizing Thomas was not going to answer any of Melissa's questions, Laura spoke instead. "Tom rarely leaves the house."

Thomas looked up from the floor to his mother with an expression of shock and anger. He beseeched her with his eyes to stop speaking, but she would not.

"At least during the day. He spends most of his time reading, or on the computer, but most nights he leaves, and—"

"*Mom.*" Laura stopped.

"Leaves and what?" Melissa asked.

The storm continued to rage, and the temperature remained trapped in the walls of the house. Melissa stared at Thomas, but he still would not speak. He would not meet her gaze. Melissa grew agitated. He could hear it in her voice.

"Two years. I haven't seen or heard from you in two years, and you don't even have the decency to look me in the eye?"

Thomas's face remained expressionless as he stared at the basement floor. He could tell she was hurt, but still he did nothing.

"You should have just left me on the sidewalk. I would have taken my chances with the Clouds."

There was hurt and anger in Melissa's voice. Laura spoke. "He runs."

"*Mom!*"

"Tom—she's your friend."

Annoyed, Thomas left the room and went up the stairs a few steps until he was out of sight. He sat out of their view but not out of earshot.

Afraid of the storm above, Melissa called for him to return. Laura Charon simply sighed and looked at the empty seat her son had vacated. "Let him go, Melissa."

"But the Outage, the lightning. Aren't you afraid of what could happen?"

"I am, but he's not. Not anymore."

"You mean after his dad died, right? I remember that day." Melissa stared at the floor.

"I forgot you were there. He still runs in them, you know?"

"In the storms?"

Laura nodded, a look of complacency and patience on her face.

"But they're dangerous. And you still let him?"

"How can I stop him? It's the only time he feels he can be alone."

Melissa looked toward the stairs, sad for her high school friend.

"Late at night I hear him leave the house," Laura went on. "After a few hours he comes back sweating and out of breath. Whether there's an Outage or not, he runs."

Melissa kept her eyes on the stairs. "Why does he run so late?"

"I don't know for sure, and when I ask he won't tell me, but I think it's to make sure things like this don't happen."

"Things like what?"

"Like running into people from high school. Old friends like you."

Melissa turned back to Laura. "Why?"

"He doesn't want to have to explain what he's been doing for two years. He doesn't want to have to tell them he never went to college. I don't think he wants them to look at him differently, like he's broken.

"You see, after Charles . . . died, something happened to Tom. He lost something. He stopped believing in things the way he used to. I guess you could say he grew up, but he's not the same person he used to be. After Charles gave up, so did Tom—only Tom kept breathing. But he hasn't given up completely. He won't say it, but I can tell he's trying to figure things out, find his way. Most days he stays in the house, reads. I think the only reason he left the house today was because he heard a storm was moving this way."

"But it's been two years."

"Charles changed the way he looked at things, and I don't even think Tom knows why."

The two women fell silent. Thomas sat on the stairs, waiting for the storm to pass, letting his mind wander to nights as he and Melissa enjoyed looking up into the clear night sky at the full moon and the stars.

"I can't remember the last time I saw the sky so clear," said Melissa

"I can't remember the last time I even saw the sky, with all these Outages happening lately. They seem to be occurring more often, and the Clouds seem to be getting larger."

Holding her hand to her mouth, Melissa began to cough. She couldn't stop. Thomas sat up and looked at her, concerned. "Are you okay?" he asked

She quit coughing and ignored the question as she pointed at the moon. " See the rabbit?"

"What?"

She kept pointing. "The rabbit in the moon. Do you see it?" Thomas laid back and shook his head. "Turn your head to the side."

She cocked her head to the right and began outlining the inner craters of the moon. "See it now? There are the ears, there's the head, and there's the body. A rabbit. See?"

Both stared at the sky, heads cocked to the right. "You don't see it do you?"

"No."

Melissa laughed. "Then what do you see, Charon?"

"Well, there's the Mare Cognitum, the Mare Imbrium, the Copernicus Crater, the Mare Serenitatis, the Mare Tranquillitatis, and the Mare Fecunditatis." He kept looking at the moon while Melissa wore a blank stare and looked at him.

Feeling her eyes on him, he turned. "What?"

"You don't see a rabbit, but you can name all the locations on the moon's surface? I thought you were a computer nerd."

"I remember it from high school."

"You really need to stop reading."

Thomas smiled. Before he could react, Melissa leaned over and placed her lips to his. Quickly pulling away, she laid her head to his chest as his body began to shake.

"Mel, I—"

"Shut up, Tom, and look at the stars." She wrapped her arms around his waist and smiled.

Thomas, enjoying the moment, cleared his mind and thought of the afternoon sky through the double glass doors of the high school two years earlier, reassembling the reality of the world from open air to enclosed walls. His mother's car approached. As it pulled up next to the building, he stepped to the car, opened the door, and sat. His mother was gripping the wheel. He closed the door and letting his book bag rest between his legs. She accelerated forward, past the intersection into the street.

"Mom? What happened? What's wrong? I was just told to get my books and meet you outside the school."

Her eyes glistened. "There's been an accident."

Tears streamed from her eyes. She did not wipe them away as they approached the hospital emergency. Sirens and lights competed with the ringing of his phone from a night in the future. He picked up the phone and heard his mother's voice.

"Tom?"

"Hey, Mom. What's up?"

"It's Melissa."

His heart skipped a beat. He sat up in bed. "What? What's wrong? Is she okay?"

"Yes. She's fine. We're at the hospital."

"What happened?"

"She was having trouble breathing and she couldn't stop coughing, so she called and asked me to take her to the hospital."

Thomas began putting on his coat. "Where was her aunt?"

"At home."

"Why didn't she take her?"

"She said she needed gas money."

Thomas paused before tying his right shoe. He could hear the agitation in his mother's voice. "*What?*"

"I know—I said the same thing. And according to Melissa, her aunt is threatening to kick her out unless she gets money for rent."

"But she has cancer. How is she supposed to pay rent when she can barely stand?" Thomas grabbed his keys and walked out the door of his apartment.

"I know. I thought it was ridiculous too."

"We've got to get her out of there."

"I was thinking the same thing. What do you think about Melissa coming to stay with us when she gets out of the hospital?"

Thomas walked into the parking lot. "It's fine with me if it's okay with you. I'll be here studying most of the time so it's really your decision."

"You'd be okay with that?"

"She spends most of her time over at the house anyway. I don't see why not."

"Good, because I've already asked and she said yes."

Thomas smiled as he opened his car door. "How is she now?"

"Fine. Resting."

"Okay. I'm in the car now. I'll be there in about an hour and a half."

"Okay, Sweetheart. I'll see you soon. And drive safe."

Thomas hung up the phone, started the engine, and listened to the engine idle as the vision cleared to reveal Melissa's window. He knocked softly on the pane.

The room remained silent, dark, but Thomas could make out the white sheets on the bed and the outline of her body.

The walls were pink and bare of posters or pictures. All Thomas could see from his vantage point was a tack board of soccer and track medals in the corner.

The twin bed was against the wall in the left corner of the room. A mid-sized dresser was on the right between the door and closet. There were no stuffed animals or television. Everything was in the same place it used to be. Nothing had changed.

Thomas knocked again, louder. Startled, Melissa looked up.

Confused and surprised, she lifted the blanket, walked to the window, and opened it. "Tom?" she asked, half asleep. "What are you doing here? Why are you at my window?"

"I didn't want to wake your aunt."

She rubbed the sleep away from her eyes. They spoke in whispers. "What do you want?"

"I'm sorry."

She looked at him with only one eye open as she rubbed the other. "What?"

"I'm sorry for the way I acted before. I didn't mean to be rude—it's just I didn't know what to say or do. You just sort of showed up, and—"

"Tom—it's one-thirty in the morning. You couldn't tell me all this in the light of day?"

He gave a small smile. "I was in the neighborhood."

"Get in here." Melissa stepped back from the window to her bed and sat as Thomas climbed through the window, sweat dripping from his face to the floor.

Once inside, he closed the window and leaned against the sill. "I haven't done that since high school," he said, smiling.

"I haven't let anyone do that since you did it in high school." Melissa smiled. Thomas stood awkwardly, unsure of what to say. "Sit," she said to him.

"I don't want to get your sheets sweaty."

Melissa nodded. "So . . . what's up?"

Thomas was unsure of what to say, or do with his hands. His eyes probed the shadows of her room and settled on her toned thighs and tight tank top. He began to sweat profusely.

"Do you need a towel?"

Thomas realized he was staring and immediately diverted his eyes to another part of the room, avoiding her eyes and her smile. He wished he was not wearing thin running shorts. "No . . . no, I'm fine." He cleared his voice. "I only came by to apologize for the way I acted earlier today in my basement."

Melissa laughed. "You really *have* been locked in your room for two years, haven't you, Charon?" Her expression quickly changed to one of regret when she saw the look of hurt on his face.

"Forget it. Sorry I woke you." He turned to reopen the window.

She quickly moved to the other side of the room. "No! Tom—I'm sorry. I didn't mean it." She stepped in front of the window, blocking his escape. He tried to move around her. "You can't leave."

"Move, Mel—I have to go."

"Not until you promise to hang out with me later this week."

"Fine."

"You promise?"

"Yeah, I promise. Now move."

Melissa stepped away from the window. Thomas lifted it and stepped out into the night. Before he could run away, she called in a loud whisper from the window. "Tom." He turned. "It's good to see you again."

Thomas turned and ran into his mother's room, turning on the light. Startled, Laura Charon sat up in bed, squinting from the light. "Mom?" he said.

"What? Is it an Outage?"

"No, Mom—I want to talk to you about Dad's insurance money."

Thomas sat on the edge of her bed, dripping sweat into the sheets. She sat up, more concerned with the sheets than his words. "Tom, you're soaked."

"I need to know if I can use it."

Her eyes finally adjusted to the light, Laura opened her eyes wide enough to see the stern expression on her son's face. She straightened and placed her hands on top of the sheets. "For what?"

"Melissa. She has cancer and needs treatment."

Thomas's words knocked her back to the headboard and left her unsure of what to say. "Tom—"

"She needs help and can't afford it on her own. Her aunt won't help. You remember the way she used to be when Melissa was in high school. I know the insurance won't pay for it all, but it will help. I know I said I would never use it, but it's not for me. It's for Mel."

Sitting on the edge of the bed, his face drenched in sweat, his eyes pleaded for an answer. She sat, exhaustion gone from her face, eyes alert. The house was filled with silence, with nothing but the sounds of breathing filling the dead air.

Laura smiled. "I think that would be a great idea." A smile lit Thomas's face. "And tell her if she needs anything from us, a place to stay, anything, all she has to do is ask."

Thomas wrapped his arms around his mother, drenching her in sweat.

"Tom!"

"Sorry." He kissed her on the cheek, turned off the light, closed the door, and went down the stairs, where he found sunlight shining through the windows of the foyer, lighting the hall to the kitchen, illuminating the cupboards and connecting one memory to the other.

Thomas filled a glass with water. Beside the sink was a letter addressed to him. Opening the envelope, he leaned against the counter, drank, and read by the sun shining through closed windows.

"What's that?" Melissa asked as she entered the kitchen, coughing. Thomas crumpled the letter and threw it in the trash.

"Nothing. Are you okay?"

"Yeah, just need some water."

Before approaching the sink, Melissa went to the trash, dripping sweat from her chin to the floor, and removed the letter.

"I threw that away for a reason."

"And I'm reading it for a reason," she said as she flattened the crumpled edges of the letter. "It's from State College." Thomas sat down at the kitchen table, saying nothing.

Melissa read, sweat speckling the page. "It says they're offering you back your scholarship. Full tuition. What's wrong with you? Why did you throw this away? You have to respond."

Thomas shrugged, taking another sip from his glass. "What's the point?"

"What's the point? It's a full academic scholarship in mathematics and computer science, and you're asking me what's the point? Most people would kill for this opportunity. I would kill for this opportunity!"

"Why don't you?"

"What?" Melissa stared at Thomas, confused.

Thomas took a drink. "If you want it so bad, you take it."

"They're not offering it to me." She began to cough.

"But they could."

She turned to the sink, pulled a glass from the cupboard, and filled a glass with water, drowning the cough and attempting to catch her breath.

"Are you sure you're okay?"

Melissa said nothing. Instead, she drank the water, set the glass on the counter, and caught her breath. Smiling, she turned and crossed her arms, but her face was tired and drained.

"Why didn't you apply to college?" Thomas asked.

Melissa's smile faded. She turned to the sink and got another glass of water. "What do you mean?" she asked, her back to Thomas.

"I mean, you're not stupid. You got almost straight A's in high school—at least while I was there. You worked hard, you did enough extra-curriculars to get some attention. I'm sure you could pay for college with scholarships if you wanted to."

Melissa took a sip of water and sat down opposite Thomas. A fake smile spread across her face. "Let's talk about something else.'

"No. It's something I've been wondering about." Thomas placed his arms on the table, leaning forward. "You know my story. What's yours? Why aren't you going to college in the fall?"

"I don't want to talk about it, Tom."

The smile was gone from her face.

"But . . ."

Melissa finished her water, stood up, and walked to the sink. "I have to go. Thanks for going running with me. Hopefully I didn't slow you down too much."

"Mel."

"I'll call you later."

"Mel, wait—"

Melissa walked down the hall and out the front door. Thomas stood slowly and walked past open doors, drawn curtains, and the bedridden patients that replaced the windows and halls of his house.

There were no screams of agony or moans of pain, only the white noise of unwatched televisions and labored breathing. Walls were filled with soothing paintings and photos of gardens, flowers, and summer days that seemed distant and unbelievable.

Thomas approached room 327. Fear of the approaching moment pulsed through his body, making him pause just outside the door. Taking a deep breath, he entered.

Laura Charon sat beside the bed, tears streaming down her face. Looking at Thomas as he entered, she did not smile.

Thomas stood still, silent. He did not want to approach, but he did. With slow, small, calculated steps, he stepped to the bed where his father lay.

Looking down, he could see his father's right leg, fully exposed and intact. His left leg was a bandaged stump, severed just below the knee. Blood stained the white bandage.

A white, paper-thin gown concealed bruises across the remainder of his body. White gauze covered the purple and black of his right eye. The other was closed.

Thomas stood silently beside the still body his father, staring at the man he admired above all others.

Laura stared at her son. She did not wipe away tears as she spoke. "The doctors say his eye will heal. There was a lot of internal bleeding when they brought him in, which they were able to stop in surgery, but his leg was too badly damaged."

Thomas stood beside the bed, unable to believe the man before him was his father. Tears welled in his eyes, blurring his vision. He closed his eyes and darkness fell. Two tears fell from his eyes, streaking his cheeks. The pain and sadness were too much to bear.

Thomas opened his eyes to the enveloping darkness of night, the image of a sleeping Melissa Pomene, and the closed window of her room. Thomas knocked twice.

"Melissa," he whispered as loud as he could. She opened her eyes and looked in his direction. Thomas smiled. She did not.

Melissa came to the window and lifted. "What is it, Tom? Here to apologize again?"

"Come with me?"

"What? Where?"

Melissa stepped back as Thomas climbed through the window.

"To college," he said, standing up.

Melissa closed the window. "Be quiet," she whispered.

"Sorry."

They went to the bed and sat. "Come with me to college," Thomas said again. "I'm sure you can get a scholarship, and if we get everything turned in on time, we could be enrolled for fall semester."

"Tom . . ." She stood up, rubbing the sides of her head and looking out the window.

"If money is an issue, I can help."

"Tom . . ." She faced the window, away from Tom.

"Because I have money from my dad's life insurance that was left to me after the settlement—"

"Tom, I have cancer."

She turned to him. His face was a mask of loss. "*What?*"

"I have cancer. Ovarian. And according to the doctors, it's spread to my lungs."

Thomas sat on the bed and looked at the floor, trying to make sense of it all. "When did this happen? When did you find out?"

She walked back to the bed and sat next to him. "Senior year."

"But . . . why didn't you tell me?"

"How could I? I hadn't heard from you since I thought you left for college. I wrote, called, but you wouldn't return my messages, so I gave up."

He began to connect the dots. "The coughing . . ."

Melissa nodded.

"But what are you doing about it? What kind of treatment are you getting?"

She sighed. "Mel?"

"I'm not receiving treatment."

"What do you mean, you're not getting treatment?"

"Why should I?" She snapped.

The harshness in her voice threw him off balance. "Because?"

"Because what? Because I have people who care about me? Like a father I never met, or a mother who cared enough about me to leave me with an aunt who could give two shits about me? I'm sorry, Tom, but I'm not you."

"But—"

"No, Tom—I'm done. I've been fighting all my life. You know better than anyone, and I'm tired of it. When you left, I had to deal with the reality of this place. Sure I thought of going to college and getting out of a crappy life I had no say so in, but all those dreams went out the window when I got sick. So I just decided to accept it. Besides, I have no way to pay for cancer treatments. I can't even pay for the tests they ran on me."

Without hesitation, Thomas said, "I can help."

Melissa's look of anger became one of sarcasm. She began to laugh. He was hurt, but he tried not to show it. "You? Right. How would you do that, Tom?"

"With the insurance money I was talking about."

"I don't think so."

Melissa stood and walked to the window, the sarcastic smile still on her face. Thomas placed his head in his hands, frustrated, then looked up. "You have to do something!"

"No, Tom, *you* have to do something." She looked at him. "You have to get out of your mother's house."

"We're not talking about that, Mel. Don't change the subject."

"You're too smart to stay around here."

"I hate it when people say that. And I'm not going anywhere."

"There's nothing you can do here."

"I can stay with you."

"You can't stay with me. Have you seen the size of this room? And besides, I don't think my aunt would like you living here. She doesn't even like *me* living here."

"Stop joking around—this is serious," he said. Melissa shook her head and smiled. "Fine. If you won't get treatment than I don't have to go to college."

Melissa paused, unsure of what to say. Believing it was a joke she began to giggle. "Tom—"

"No—I'm serious." Melissa stopped smiling. "If you aren't going to get treatment for your cancer, then I'm not going to college. It's as simple as that."

Thomas stood and crossed his arms. He looked at Melissa, having made up his mind.

"You have no idea what you're talking about."

"I know plenty."

"Tom—"

"Unless you agree to treat your cancer, I stay here."

Melissa heaved a heavy sigh, walked past Thomas, and sat on the edge of the bed. He stood in front of the window, his arms still crossed. Melissa looked at his stern expression and gave a soft chuckle.

He couldn't help cracking a smile. He knew he looked ridiculous.

"And if I get help?"

"If you get help, I go."

She gave another sigh. "You're out of your mind. You know that, right?"

Thomas smiled, and Melissa began to cough, filling the room with the harsh sound. Each articulation separated into different voices, tones, and muffled laughter of friends and family as the room expanded on all sides, pushing apart bed and walls, connecting the endless oblivion of his thoughts. Faded grass grew from dingy carpet, and sunlight shined through bare tree branches that filled the backyard home of Mr. and Mrs. Charles Charon. Thomas walked with a bag of ice, passing guests, friends, and family as they moved from outside to in, and back out, with plates filled with barbecued meats and side items.

He dumped the bag of ice into the red-and-white cooler, covering the warm sodas. The smell of chicken, hamburgers, and ribs filled the air. Everyone congratulated him as he passed by, searching for his mother. She stood at the grill, cooking.

"Mom, where's Dad? I thought he was cooking today."

"He went upstairs for a minute. He wasn't feeling well."

Thomas was overcome by fear, his smile wiped by dread. He looked at the sky. In the distance, lightning flash from sky to ground.

"Tom?"

"Mom, get everyone inside."

"What's wrong?"

"It's an Outage."

Laura looked to the sky and saw for herself.

"Everyone!" Thomas yelled to friends and family standing in the backyard. "We all need to get inside the house as quickly as possible."

Everyone looked at him, confused. Melissa, standing nearby, made her way to him. "Tom, what's wrong? What's going on?"

"Mel, it's an Outage. Get inside."

"But, where are the . . ."

As if answering her question, Sirens filled the air—and everyone immediately understood the threat and walked to the doors. Thomas pushed his way past the guests, making his way to the steps.

"Tom, what's wrong?" He could hear Melissa's voice, but he did not answer. He continued to climb two steps at a time to reach his parents' room.

Below, the guests were calm and quiet. Outside, Sirens continued to fill the air. Thomas ran to the door of his parents' room. Without knocking, he opened the door and found the room empty. His father's prosthetic leg lay on the carpeted floor. Before he could step inside, the sound of a gun reverberated throughout the house.

Thomas jumped. Someone screamed downstairs. The house went silent, as did the Sirens.

Thomas raced to the bathroom. Opening the door, he looked down and saw his father hunched near the toilet, a bullet hole in his temple.

Blood was already pooling around pills and an open bottle that were scattered on the floor. Blood was running down his neck from the wound to the floor. A gun lay beside his lifeless hand. The room still smelled of lavender—his mother's favorite.

Thomas slowly stepped into the room and knelt in the blood beside his father. There was no life in his father's eyes.

"Tom? What was—" Laura walked in and immediately dropped to her knees.

She shook her head in disbelief. "No. No, no, *no* . . ." She fell against the wall and slid to the floor.

Thomas kneeled there for moments, listening to his mother's sobs and the silence from the crowd below. Finally, without speaking or crying, he stood. Clothes and hands covered in blood, he walked past his mother out the door and toward the stairs.

Guests, friends, and family all parted as Thomas passed.

"Tom?" Melissa said.

He opened the front door, stepped onto the porch, and began to run.

"Tom!" Melissa called through the crowd.

Ignoring her calls, Thomas ran out the door and into the night-filled day of Clouds before entering Melissa Pomene's hospital room.

Melissa looked out the window at the Clouds. Rain dripped down the window. Her complexion was white, lips purple, and auburn hair thin. She looked at the door and forced a smile. "Hey you."

Her voice was soft, raspy. Thomas didn't smile as he approached. When she tried to sit up, he hurried to her bedside, but she pushed him back.

"Can you close the door?" Thomas walked back and closed the door. "Lock it."

He locked the handle without question before walking back to her bedside. "How are you feeling?" he asked.

Melissa tried to smile. "Wonderful."

"Mel—"

"Stop worrying so much about me, Charon, and sit down. You're making me nervous."

Thomas pulled a chair beside the bed. "Not there. Here. I want you beside me."

Thomas sat on the edge of the bed. Taking her hand in one of his, he touched the side of her face with his other one. She closed her eyes at his touch. Her skin was smooth and warm under his fingertips.

"That's nice," she said. Thomas gave her half a smile.

."Come here, " Melissa said. She took her hand from his and grabbed his shirt, pulling him down with as much force as she could. She opened her eyes.

Thomas bent forward. She wrapped her arms around his back and placed her lips to his. Uncomfortable, he kissed her as best he could. Then, taking one hand from his back, she began to unzip his pants.

Thomas pulled away and stood up. "What are you doing?"

She tried to pull him back to her, but could not.

"Melissa, stop. You're too weak. We shouldn't be doing this."

He zipped his pants as she looked back to the window. "What?" he asked.

She said nothing.

"Mel, I—"

"I'm dying, Tom." She turned from the window. "Truly dying. Do you know what that's like?"

Thomas remained silent.

"No—you don't. But I don't expect you to. I don't want you to. I hope to God you never have to. But what I do want is to not feel like I'm dying. Just for a while. Just for a few minutes. I can deal with the fact that I'm going to die if you wouldn't pull away from me every time I try to even touch you. Death isn't contagious."

"I know that."

"Then what's the problem?"

"It's just . . ." Thomas paused, hesitant.

"What—you're afraid you're going to break me?"

"Yeah . . . sort of . . . I don't know."

"Well let me assure you, Charon, I am *not* going to break." She attempted to smile, then began to cough. Taking a sip of water from the cup on the nightstand, she laid down, exhausted. Thomas remained standing and still.

"Don't look at me like that," she said.

"Like what?"

"Like I'm already dead." Melissa turned back toward the window. Not knowing what to say, Thomas remained silent as tears fell from the corners of her eyes. The only sound was the rain hitting the window.

He walked to the bed, sat on the edge, and wiped away her tears. At his touch, she broke down and sobbed softly. She continued to cry as he pulled back her blanket. Cupping her head in his hands, he kissed her softly as she moved her hands to the bottom of his shirt to pull it over his head. Her tears continued to fall as Thomas opened his eyes to a light shining down from Pandora's ceiling. He wasn't sure where he was or how he got there. He searched his thoughts, but remembered nothing—as if his memories had been erased.

❊ ❊ ❊

Thomas Charon lay on the floor on his back, staring into the white light. A stream of blood and tears ran down both cheeks from his nose and eyes, forming a small pool on the white-tiled floor beneath his head. His eyes fluttered shut.

He rolled to his side, sending waves of pain radiating throughout his head and causing his eyesight to blur. His eyes scanned the room, but he was unable to focus on a single object. Nothing looked familiar. His eyes went in and out of focus as he searched for an explanation of why he was lying on the floor of a white room with blood running from his nose. There was not a clue.

He looked left and right, from the bed to the dresser to the wall, but saw nothing that triggered a single memory.

Behind him were two red halos and the foggy image of a body a few feet away. Using what little strength he had, he crawled to the side of the person he now recognized, her eyes focused on the ceiling, unblinking, still.

He tentatively touched her pale flesh, wincing in pain as images of locales, people, and random events bombarded his mind in an array of colors, removed from the logical sequence of time. Thomas placed his hand to her face and sensed the name "Remus."

Drops of blood fell from his nose. He opened his eyes and swallowed, and managed a soft, raspy whisper: "Wait—be . . . back."

Lacking the strength to walk, Thomas crawled toward the open door and the kitchen, sensing he knew where to go and where he was, but unsure how he knew. After touching the woman's cheek, he became aware he was in a place called "Pandora," but nothing else. He couldn't remember how or why he got there or what it was—let alone the year.

Crawling along the floor, Thomas felt as if his muscles and limbs had not been used in months. Reaching the door, he used the handle to pull himself to feet that didn't feel like his own. Opening the door, he stumbled to the sink, turned on the faucet, and placed his head beneath the spigot, sucking in water with exhausted gulps.

Eyes closed, Thomas focused on the water. The moment was drowned by the sensation of water flowing down his swollen throat. Exhaustion radiated throughout his muscles, causing him to lose strength and balance. His skull felt as if it were being split open by the magnitude of the headache. But despite all this, his thoughts somehow returned to the woman lying on the floor in a small pool of her own blood. His eyes sprang open.

Lifting his head from under the spigot, Thomas searched for a cup and found one in the sink. He filled it and shut off the faucet to save water. He knew it only dispensed a certain amount of water daily, but couldn't remember how much or how he knew. He could feel strength returning to his legs and arms as he carefully carried the cup back to the woman still unmoving on the floor.

He knelt beside her still body and placed one hand behind her head, tilting it toward the cup. He drizzled a little water onto her chapped lips, but her eyes remained transfixed on the ceiling as water ran down both sides of her mouth and mixed with her blood.

When she didn't swallow, Thomas set the cup on the floor and brought his hand to her face, wiping away blood with his sleeve. He placed his hand on her cheek and her name came to him. "Andrea."

His senses were bombarded with scents, tastes, touches, smells, and images of every person who'd ever said her name in her lifetime, moving from the past to the present in an illogical order. Blood ran from her nose.

Her mouth opened with a gasp that filled her lungs, causing her back to arch off the ground. Thomas stared in disbelief as she gasped for more and more air.

She turned on her side to face him as her gasps turned into dry coughs. He handed her the cup of water. After just a moment, she quit gasping but continued to cough.

"More?"

She nodded, still coughing. He hurried to the kitchen, dropped the cup in the sink, and went to the pantry, where he found some bottled water. He grabbed a bottle, rushed back to Andrea, and got her to sit up. She continued to cough and tried to catch her breath as he knelt by her side, removed the cap, and handed her the bottle. She raised it to her lips and didn't stop drinking until the bottle was empty.

She gasped again and turned to Thomas. "What happened?"

❃ ❃ ❃

Andrea sat crying on the bloodstained white tile, her knees pressed to her chest as she rocked back and forth. Thomas sat against the wall, one hand on his head, emotionally and physically drained.

She lifted her head from her knees and looked in his direction. Tears continued to stream down her cheeks. "What happened?" she asked. "Why can't I stop crying." Thomas did not meet her gaze, staring instead at the blood on the floor.

"All I have are these emotions—no memories. It's like my senses have been overloaded with every emotion I've ever felt. And why can't I remember anything?"

Thomas continued to sit in silence.

"I know something has happened, but—" Andrea pressed her hands against her temples in a desperate attempt to remember what she knew had been wiped from her mind. Tears continued to fall. "—I can't remember. Tom—why can't I remember?"

"I don't know—I don't know." He looked at her, confused. Why couldn't they remember? Why did every emotion seem to radiate throughout their bodies? All that existed were gaps, and they needed time to connect the dots.

"I need more water. I can't think straight. Come on. We'll talk more in the kitchen," said Thomas.

❋ ❋ ❋

"Let's work backwards," Thomas said after a while. "What can you remember?"

Empty water bottles littered the table between them. Andrea had stopped crying, and after scouring their brains for memories for thirty minutes, their emotions had subsided. "We've been through this, Tom. I only remember you."

"You don't remember anything else?"

"No."

"Because I remember you, but I also remember my mom and dad," he said. "But I can only remember their faces. I saw them after we touched. I didn't even know who you were before then. I woke up on the floor not knowing or remembering anything about where I was or what I was doing, but feeling as if I should know. Nothing like that happened to you? You don't remember anything?"

Andrea shook her head. "I can't remember anything. It's like you said. The memories are there, but they're hazy. I don't even know how we ended up on the floor all bloody."

Thomas stared at the empty bottles absentmindedly. "Something happened—a long time ago. I don't know how I know, but I do." Andrea said nothing.

Thomas continued to force memories to return. "Before coming here, we had a discussion and a guest. He was showing something . . . something to do with this place—and you got angry and walked out. Do you remember? We were back at home."

"No. The only thing that keeps coming to mind is a name." She paused for a moment, letting the letters form in her mind before uttering something. "Munin."

As she spoke the name, images of a man in a black suit appeared before both of them, sending waves of pain through their heads. Both winced before opening their eyes.

"What was that?" said Andrea.

"You saw it too—the man in the black suit?"

Andrea nodded. "I think that was Munin."

Thomas stood from the table and walked to the door. "Come with me."

Andrea followed him to Pandora's control room, where three screens were displayed. One held a list of names. Others displayed orbital calculations of locations throughout the galaxy. Both inspected the room as if it seeing it for the first time.

"Tom—what's this?"

Thomas stared at the screens and monitors, trying to remember details of a lucid dream that had become his life. "I've been here. We've both been here—not now, but before, years before. Something happened . . . something happened to us. In some way it's the reason for all of this."

Thomas rubbed his temples in an attempt to bring up thoughts he knew would make sense, if he could only remember them. Andrea walked around the perimeter of the room, studying the screens, the computer, the work stations. She stopped at the clock attached to the computer console.

"Tom. Come here. Look at the year. This can't be right, can it?" They both stared, confused. "That's twelve years from now."

Thomas looked at the clock, then back to the monitors. "We were arguing." He pointed at the display of names. "I found it after . . . God—it's right there, but I can't remember. All I can think of is some stupid word that begins with a P—Pa . . . Pa . . .

"Pandora."

Andrea and Thomas looked at each other. The name circulated around the room, transporting their thoughts simultaneously to twelve years earlier, explaining the circumstances leading to their placement in the Pandora facility.

Lethe

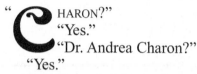

"CHARON?"

"Yes."

"Dr. Andrea Charon?"

"Yes."

"My name is Munin. I spoke to you and your husband on the phone. May I come in?"

Andrea Remus Charon stared through the partially open door of her suburban home into the expressionless eyes and face of the man standing before her. He wore a black suit, white shirt, and black tie. Neither his face nor shirt were wrinkled. His arms were at his sides. In his left hand he held a black leather briefcase. His eyes were dark. His voice and tone were calm, controlled. He did not smile, and neither did she.

They studied each other before she spoke. "Yes. Please. Come in."

He walked through the door, passing her. Closing the door, she led him from the narrow enclosed hall to the living room, with its cream painted walls and hardwood floors. Sunlight radiated through the windows from a partly cloudy afternoon sky, filling the room with natural light. A single step separated the hall, partially sunken living room, and dining area. To the left was the dining room and an open arch that led to the kitchen. Directly ahead the hall continued to closed doors—study and bedroom—and the backyard observatory.

Sitting close to the wall in a cushioned armchair was Thomas Charon. He looked up with a smile of enthusiasm as they entered. "Tom, this is Munin," Andrea said.

Standing, Thomas extended his hand in greeting, which Munin accepted. "Nice to meet you," he said. He paused for a moment, unsure of what to say next before continuing. "I have to tell you, after our conversation, Andrea and

I have been very curious to know the details of this project you talked about." Excitement was evident in his voice.

Munin said nothing, displaying no emotions. "May I sit?" he asked.

"Yes," Thomas said, surprised, caught off guard. "Yes, of course."

Sitting on the couch, Munin placed his briefcase on his knees and opened it. Andrea and Thomas sat beside each other as he removed three large manila folders from the briefcase and placed them on the coffee table. As Munin closed the case and placed it under the table, Thomas picked up the first folder and began flipping through its pages.

Each were marked with the name Pandora.

"As you know, our weather conditions have grown increasingly hostile over the last few years. Temperature fluctuations, weather anomalies, power failures. These are problems scientists like yourselves—astrophysics and computer technology and software—have been working tirelessly to remedy, with little to no success. This is why I'm here—"

"Because of the weather stabilizing device, right?" Thomas said.

Andrea sat quietly, face as hard and emotionless as the man in the black. Munin looked directly at Thomas. "What do you know about the WSD, Dr. Charon?"

"Umm, well . . . I know it's a device under construction that was created to stabilize the weather. I know it's a global initiative. Scientists everywhere, in every field, are being asked to assist in studying the Clouds, their movements, and placing the devices across the globe in the most optimal locations—hopefully to slow or stop their formation."

"What else do you know?"

Without hesitation, said, "I know some believe it won't work. But that's all hearsay."

Munin turned to Andrea Remus Charon. "What do you believe, Mrs. Charon?"

Andrea said nothing as Thomas returned his attention to the folders, continuing to flip through the pages. "Why is

Pandora written at the top of each page?" he asked. "Is that the name given to the WSD?"

"No, Dr. Charon," Munin said. "I'm not here to speak to you about the construction of the WSD. I'm here about something much more serious. I'm here seeking reassurance."

Thomas's excitement faded as confusion took over. "Reassurance?" he said. "Reassurance of what?"

"Reassurance that the problem facing our planet can be remedied when the device fails." A small cloud passed overhead, shrouding the room in temporary darkness before it moved on.

"*When* it fails? What do you mean *when* it fails?" Andrea asked, putting more emphasize on the when.

Munin adjusted his posture. "I'm sorry to inform you, Dr. Charon—the WSD is a ploy. It's a publicity stunt, as simple as that—a device to raise public spirits. That's all. The reason I'm here is to discuss the schematics you hold in your hand. Its name is Pandora. In its simplest terms, Pandora is—"

"Wait, wait, wait. Hold on for a minute." Thomas closed the folder and placed it on his lap. He closed his eyes and rubbed his head. "Let me get this straight. You're telling us that you're not here to discuss the weather stabilizing device?" Thomas leaned against the back of couch, still rubbing his head, desperately trying to make sense of it all. "You're here to talk to us about something called Pandora? What's that?"

"In its simplest terms, Pandora is an advanced computer designed to plot the course of any object from Earth's orbit to any destination in the galaxy. Pandora, the machine outlined in these folders, is an extremely sophisticated computer, containing data known to exist on all objects in our solar system, all other discovered systems, and their known movements. Creating the most detailed galactic map ever to be assembled."

"So . . . space, not Earth?" Thomas asked, leaning forward.

"Yes," Munin said with no sign of annoyance in his voice. "However, what makes Pandora special is its ability to plot the course of any object moving away from Earth with the use of the IPS, rather than conventional propulsion techniques—"

"Pandora requires using the IPS?" asked Andrea.

Munin nodded.

Still confused, Thomas looked from one to the other. "What's the IPS?"

Andrea turned to Thomas and began to explain. "It's a form of space travel called the Interplanetary Superhighway—IPS for short."

Thomas was lost, so Andrea continued. "Okay," she tried to find the best way of explaining the complex theory to her husband. "Rather than sending an object through space using a rocket and fuel, the IPS uses the gravitational pulls of other planets, stars, and asteroids to move from one location to the other. It implies the use of Lagrange movements and pockets of weak and strong gravities. So rather than moving from point A to point E, objects moving through the IPS move from point B to C to D before reaching the destination—E."

Thomas was still confused. "That makes no sense. Wouldn't using the IPS take longer?"

"Yes—and no. The use of a rocket means the use of fuel. The greater the distance, the more fuel is required, creating more weight and shortening its distance. That means it can only visit point E before having to use its remaining fuel to return. By using the IPS, the craft can visit point E, move to other points of destination, then return only using a quarter of its fuel, if any.

"Many missions in space have been implementing the IPS as the Outages have grown worse, to gather photos and samples from planets. The only problem with using it is its longevity, which you pointed out. But with the correct calculations, it's more reliable and efficient." She turned to Munin. "Am I correct?" she asked.

He nodded. "The schematic outline of Pandora you hold in your hand is designed for two people," Munin said. "The structure has been built and now needs individuals familiar with its specifics to lead in its research."

Andrea shook her head in disbelief. "But why would you need us? It doesn't make sense. I've done some research on the IPS and the use of Lagrange calculations, but I can name at least a dozen more qualified individuals who would be a better choice to lead this project. And why is Pandora so important? There are already computer programs that can assist in calculating movements throughout the IPS."

"This is true, Dr. Charon, but there is a second component to Pandora I have yet to mention, and it's why Mr. Charon's assistance is needed to monitoring the use of MR, which Pandora uses."

Andrea looked at Munin. "What's MR?"

Thomas looked up with renewed interest, confusion, and a sarcastic smile. "I'm sorry, but I'm lost. None of this fits. Why would Lagrange movements, IPS, and memory replay be needed for a space exploration?

"What's memory replay?" Andrea asked.

Munin sighed. "There is a section of the brain known as the hippocampus, where all the memories of an individual's life are stored. Pandora has the ability to access that portion of the brain and those memories."

"And do what?"

Munin and Thomas said nothing. Andrea's eyes moved from one to the other in search of answers. "And do what?" she repeated.

Thomas was the first to answer. "From what I've gathered from other computer technicians and what I've read, MR gives a person the ability to revisit memories. I'm not sure of the process, the programming, or how vivid the memories can become, but I do know the software is extremely advanced— so advanced in its design and images that it can create what some programmers have called a form of time travel."

Andrea stared into the faces of the two men. "Which is why I am confused about why it's being used for space exploration," said Thomas. "It wasn't meant to be used for space travel, but designed to help trauma victims restore portions of their lost memory after a traumatic event in a safe and secure environment. From what I can tell, there's no connection to it in relation to Pandora."

A cloud passed overhead, larger and darker than before. "Conditions are far worse than either of you know," Munin said.

Andrea and Thomas stared in anticipation at the man in black as he began to provide answers they both sought.

"You, like most, know about the dying trees and plants, and the vanishing bees. What you don't know or realize is that entire sections of forests and wetlands are dying without explanation. And not only have large portions of bee populations vanished, but other wildlife and insects have begun to disappear as well."

"You mean die."

"No—disappear. As of yet, no remains have been found to verify any animals died at all. Also, it's no longer possible to forecast the weather. Because the Clouds don't move with wind patterns, and have no predictable movement, there is no way to determine where they will go, what effect they will have, if any, or how severe the next storm might be. This means that even if we did find a way to stabilize the climate, we'd still have the problem of disappearing plant and animal life. It's because of these mounting problems that the Pandora Project was put into place—to seed another planet with human life, if or when the Earth became inhospitable."

The cloud lingered overhead. The room remained in relative darkness.

"What do you mean, 'seed' another planet with life?" asked Andrea.

Munin said nothing, waiting for them to fully grasp his words. Finally Thomas spoke: "Let me get this straight— you want to create another Earth?"

Andrea began to laugh, and her husband looked at her, missing the joke. He turned back to Munin. "What does this mean? What exactly are you telling us?"

Andrea continued to laugh. "He's telling us the world is coming to an end."

"What I'm saying is, we would like reassurance in knowing life will continue.—even if this planet does not."

Andrea stopped laughing. "I don't think you understand. What you're saying is absurd." An angry smile remained on her face. "Do you know the odds of finding another planet suitable for human life? Have you heard of the Drake Equation?"

Munin remained silent.

"The conditions on Earth are a rarity, yet to be found on any other planet. Another planet not only has to have the ability to harbor, store, and replenish water and other natural resources, but it also needs an atmosphere that provides protection from solar radiation and asteroids. Also known as the Goldilocks Zone. Finding another planet the correct distance from a hospitable sun, in an isolated portion of the galaxy, shielded from large galactic debris by an asteroid belt, and in a system with a sun like ours, is by all calculations impossible."

"Our scientist have assembled a list of possible planets—"

"No! There are no possible planets because it *is* impossible."

"Andrea, hold on—"

"No, Tom! Everything he said is probability, not fact. The Clouds, the plants, all of it. None of it is supported by substantial evidence. The weather anomalies, large portions of forests gone, disappearance of entire species, all of it is speculation. Including the possibility of exo-planets that could harbor sustainable life. Where's the proof?"

"Calm down. Let's finishing hearing what he has to say. There are still some questions that need—"

"You can finish talking. I'm done."

Andrea stood from the couch and started walking toward the back of the house.

"What's wrong with you?" Thomas said.

Andrea stopped and turned. "What's wrong with *me*? A man we never met has just come into our house and said the human race is going to end and he needs our help to ensure its survival on another planet. He listed problems that cannot be fixed, and says the best we can do now is rely on a machine named Pandora that somehow uses IPS and MR to moving materials from one side of the universe to the other. I'm sorry, Tom, but this is a little too much for me to handle in one sitting. You can stay and chit-chat, but I'm done."

Andrea turned toward the hall and walked away. Her quick, forceful footsteps echoed throughout the house and culminated with the sound of the slamming door.

Thomas turned to Munin and continued the conversation. He was calm and collected, but now he was more serious than before. "Munin, if you don't mind, I still have some questions—one of those being, why the need for MR? I can understand that Andrea and her knowledge of space and planets would be a viable asset to this project, but why the need for memory extraction in the production of Pandora?"

"As I said before, reassurance. We have the genetic material necessary to seed another planet over time. However, the necessity of making sure the memory of who and where we are as a species must be present as well. The only way to be absolutely certain that happens is to supply the memories ourselves."

Taking the folder Thomas held in his hand, Munin flipped through its pages and found the schematic details outlining Pandora. "As you can see, Pandora is connected to three screens, each wrapping from one side of the room to the other. Each screen is equipped to display multiple windows of information at once. Information such as planetary charts, information from the Extra-solar Planets Encyclopedia, or a celestial map of the region. Mostly these three monitors will be used by the individual plotting Pandora's course.

"In front of the monitors will be Andrea's and your direct link to Pandora—a computer console that you both will work from. Each will have your own work station. One will plot the course of Pandora and the other will sift and load the memories directly into the system to fill the 2,000 categories needed to represent what it means to be human. These categories range from abstract thoughts of imagination to the endurance of the human spirit. Once these memories have been carefully placed into each category, fulfilling each requirement, they will then be uploaded into Pandora in Earth's orbit, ready to be sent at a moment's notice."

"Where do these memories come from?" asked Thomas.

Munin faltered momentarily, then said, "Pandora is like no other machine created in the fact that it can't be controlled."

"What do you mean 'can't be controlled'?" Thomas asked, concerned.

"Rather than turn on and off at the command of individuals like you or me and remain disconnected from its operators like most other machines, Pandora does not shut down until it has completed its task, no matter how long it may take. What I explained to you is true, that one individual is required to plot Pandora's course while the other loads the collected, but when the two individuals working on the device walk away from Pandora, whether for a few hours or a few minutes, Pandora does not shut down. Rather, it continues to build a relationship between itself and the two individuals at its controls."

"I'm not sure I understand what you mean by 'build a relationship.' How is that possible? It's only a machine."

"It is more than just a machine, Dr. Charon—much more." Munin looked directly in Thomas's eyes to drive home the point. "If you and your wife agree to participate in the project, the memories used by Pandora will be gathered from the two of you when you aren't working on the machine. Pandora is designed to plot the course of any object we choose to send from Earth, but when you aren't in direct contact with Pandora, when your fingertips are not directly on the keyboard, or your mind focused on the task on the screens and monitors, it will be extracting memories from the both of you to be stored for later use. To accomplish this, Pandora detects frequencies in the hippocampus of the brain only given off when it is at rest, giving it the opportunity to recall memories from the past. When Pandora detects the memory it needs, it copies the memory from the original. However, to make a copy of the original memory it must replay the thought, making the mind believe the memory is being experienced for the first time."

Thomas was at a loss for words, trying to articulate questions that eluded him. The man in black tried to put his explanation into an example he could understand. "Think of the first time you had ice cream. It may be difficult to recall, but it is stored in your memory. Pandora accesses that portion of your brain, and makes a copy of the memory. However, when this occurs, it fools your mind into believing you are the same age you were when you had your first ice cream. Pandora takes individuals back to that exact moment and makes them believe they are actually there for the first time."

"So let me get this straight," Thomas said. "Pandora has the ability to take me back to the moment when I had my first ice cream and allow me to taste the flavor I had?"

"Not only that, but you'd be able to see the same images, hear the same sounds, and even experience the same joy you experienced from the taste. Pandora transports the individual back, completely, to everything present, around, and inside themselves during the memory. Pandora is designed to identify and store these feelings of happiness, pain, sorrow, joy, ecstasy, love, and fear . They are what it means to be human and are what will be used for the continuation of our species, if it comes to that.

Thomas looked at the folders on the coffee table with a blank stare. "This means we can relive our happiest memories—or our worse nightmares—as if for the first time." He kept his eyes on the manila folders. "Tell me, Mr. Munin— will the feelings we experience in these memory replays carry over to how we feel in the present?"

"If you're asking, will you remember the memory replays as if you just experienced the memories all over again, the answer is yes. And as you work on Pandora, the memories will become stronger and more vivid."

"More vivid? What do you mean?"

"As you continue to work on Pandora, you'll find it develops a stronger relationship between you and itself. It learns, grows, and becomes just as curious as any other intelligence. This means the longer you remain in direct contact with it, the stronger and longer the memory replays will become. In many ways, it's a side-effect of the device. One that we've been unable to remedy."

"What does that mean for Andrea and me, if we agree to be a part of the project?"

"It means that if you work in the confines of the complex for too long, your brain will not be able to differentiate past from present, causing your mind to become lost."

Thomas's expression did not change. His eyes remained on the manila folders. "It *is* a time machine—just one we can't control but might possibly lose ourselves in."

Munin hesitated for a moment before continuing. "Dr. Charon, I know I've bombarded you with a lot of information in a short time. You need time to process it all. It's for this reason I'm leaving the two of you to think over my proposal. The information on Pandora in those folders is for you and your wife to look over and discuss.

"However, I must tell you, the need for confidentiality is of the utmost priority. The government has taken great precautions to maintain secrecy of this project, and if it was leaked that the government was putting into action plans to preserve the continuity of our species, there would be severe repercussions—and the government would deny all knowledge of this conversation. Is that understood?"

Thomas nodded.

Reassured that Dr. Charon knew and understood the possible consequences, Munin retrieved his briefcase from the floor and stood. Thomas stood as well.

"Understand the necessity of this project, Dr. Charon, and what your assistance means. Look over the material and make your decision wisely. I'll be in contact soon."

Without saying another word, Munin walked to the hall, leaving Thomas alone, lost in thought.

After Munin closed the front door, Thomas fell on the couch, feeling nauseous. He rubbed his temples and leaned back, trying to clear his mind. Nothing made sense.

Lost, he opened his eyes and looked at the four folders on the coffee table. He picked up the top one and began to read.

Thomas read the confidential pages by the light coming through the living room windows. He read how memories were copied from the hippocampus, the scarring that occurred after extended use, the process of dividing the memories into the categories needing to be filled, side effects of headaches, nose bleeds after prolonged exposure, and the eventual loss of time comprehension. With each new page, Munin's words were verified. His stomach was twisted in knots, making it difficult to breathe.

An hour passed since Munin left, and Andrea had not returned.

Thomas closed the folder and put it on the table with the others. Standing, he heaved a heavy sigh, as if he'd been holding his breath since Munin's departure. His mind wandered from thought to thought, searching for an anchor to ground his swimming emotions. He thought of implications of what Pandora and its creation meant.

Collecting his composure, Thomas went to the back door. Opening it, he walked toward the woman he'd grown so accustomed to since their marriage—Andrea, looking through their telescope into the now clear sky as twilight neared.

He approached her feeling lost and unsure of what to say, but he forced a smile, trying to pretend everything was normal. She did not look up. "So, who was Pandora?" he asked.

Andrea took her eyes off the sky and looked at her husband's smiling face. "What?"

"I've skimmed through most of pages in a few of the folders, but I can't find anything explaining who Pandora was. I know she was a woman, and it has something to do with mythology, but that's all."

"You know how to design and reconfigure advanced computer software with ease, but you don't know the story of Pandora?"

Thomas shrugged. "I must have skipped that day in high school."

Annoyed, Andrea shifted her eyes back to the sky. While her head was down, Thomas dropped his pretense and let his fear of the days ahead wash over his face.

Head down and eyes to the sky, she spoke. "According to Roman mythology, there were five ages of man. The first was the golden age. In this age there were mortals, but they lived like gods. They did not have the problems we have today. They lived without sadness, sorrow, or pain. However, when they all passed away, their children inherited the Earth, creating the silver age of man. These mortals were inferior to the first in intelligence, and preservation as they continued to find new, better ways to kill and hurt one another rather than maintain peace. War became their sole reason for living—until the third and final stage of man, the bronze age. These men were strong, and had such a love for war that they were completely destroyed by their own hands.

"However, from these men were born heroes who fought wars, had epic adventures, and were the essence of stories that would define the final age of man—the iron age. They lived in evil times, and their nature was corrupt in too many ways to count. As generations continued they grew worse, and the only factor that mattered in their lives was their power and how to abuse it."

Andrea continued to look to the sky. Thomas said nothing as he waited. "What does this have to do with Pandora?"

"It was after the golden age of man that Jupiter created the first woman, Pandora, as punishment."

"Punishment for what? Sounds like they were the only ones who had it figured out."

"For the gift of fire, given to them by Prometheus, one of the few Titans allowed to remain on Earth when Jupiter defeated Kronos."

"Fire? They were punished for the gift of fire? Really?"

"Tom, do you want to hear this or not?" Andrea asked, looking up from the telescope.

Thomas said nothing. She returned to the telescope and continued. "Pandora is said to be the cause of all misfortunes in the world. Jupiter created her with great beauty, lavished her with gifts, and gave her all she could ever ask for. However, what he did not give her was a companion. Jupiter sent her to Earth and placed her in a temple alone with all she could ever ask for, and a box she was not to open at any cost. Alone in the temple, with no others to talk to, Pandora's curiosity and loneliness got the best of her. In search of a companion, Pandora opened the chest and unleashed Sickness, Disease, Sorrow, Jealousy, Hatred—all the plagues of human nature into the world. Pandora tried to close the box, but it was too late. Everything had been released, and Jupiter had gotten his revenge on man."

Andrea kept her eyes on the sky, continuing the story without emotion. "However, as Pandora cried beside the chest, saddened by what she had done, there was something she had overlooked at the bottom. Emerging, small and slow, was Hope, the only goodness in the confines of the box. It flew away with all the others, leaving Pandora to fulfill the meaning of her name—'the gift of all.'"

Andrea looked up at Thomas. He no longer had the strength to hide behind a false smile. "We need to talk," he said.

"There's nothing to talk about, Tom. I'm not doing it." She began walking across the lawn toward the house.

"Are you really going to turn your back on this?" She did not answer. "At least look at the plans."

Still Andrea said nothing. She kept walking. "Something's happening," he said. Andrea stopped before reaching the door. "You can't deny that."

She faced the house, her back was to him. "You may not have wanted to hear what Munin had to say, but you know he was right. Something is happening. It's true, some of what he said was speculation, but you know something's wrong. You feel it, just as I do. All I ask is for you to think about it. Look through the plans. Get a feel for what this is really about, and how it may be bigger than you understand."

Andrea remained still as night fell around them, darkening the sky. Without speaking, Andrea walked into the house, leaving Thomas alone beneath the first white stars. It was going to be a clear night.

Later, neither spoke. As they lay in bed, trying to sleep, both felt the weight of the world on their shoulders. Andrea lay on her back, staring into the ceiling. Thomas lay on his side, staring at the wall. The air was heavy, stale, and silent.

"How is it like time travel?" she asked.

Thomas turned toward her. "What?"

"You said memory replay was like time travel when we were talking to Munin. How? Isn't time travel impossible?"

Unsure of how to answer, he lay still, thinking. Finally he said, "It's hard to explain." He turned to face her.

She continued looking at the ceiling. "Try."

"Well, think of time as a river that never stops flowing," he said. "Downstream is the future, upstream is the past. We move along its current, floating, unable to move to the past, or jump to the future, but always remaining in the present. However, according to physics, the concept of time travel is possible."

"If it were possible, then why can't we jump back and forth from one time period to the next, moving from the present, to the future and, to the past whenever we want?"

"That's where it gets tricky. According to classic physics, traveling to the past is only possible. Not the future. So, it is true that time travel into the future is impossible, but there is no scientific explanation as to why moving backwards in time is not possible."

"Why?" she asked.

"I don't know. It's just the laws of physics."

"Then why can't we travel to the past?"

"Some believe it may have something to do with our perception of time," he said, "but for the most part it's just one of those things we don't know."

"So how is memory replay like time travel?"

"Because memories are the past. Traveling back to those memories is like jumping back in the stream."

"To a past that can't be changed," she said.

Thomas lay silent, staring at Andrea's profile in the darkness of their bedroom even as he felt his mind return to his body and the well-lit Pandora control room of Pandora twelve years in the future, with a rush of blood to his head.

"The past never changes," said Thomas.

Andrea paced from one side of the room to the other. Thomas stood still, feeling disoriented, although it seemed a portion of his memory had returned. "Why did that happen? What's going on?" she asked.

She continued to pace from one side of the room to the other. "I saw him," she said. "I saw everything. I saw Munin, the folders, our house, everything. Even the part of the conversation between Munin and your after I had left and gone outside. I saw it all as if I were actually there. As if I were you. I felt your emotions, your stress, your apprehension, but I also felt my own at the same time. I can't describe it, but—" She paused, her gaze focused directly ahead.

"What?"

"I still can't remember everything," she said. "Can you?"

Thomas searched his memory, replaying the restored memories and remembering the feelings of fear after the visit of Munin, but couldn't remember what came next. "No."

Fear spread across Andrea's face as she looked into his eyes. "Tom, what's happening? It's like there's a gap in my memory. Some of it's been filled, but the only thing that's coming to mind are those damn—"

Unable to finish, she found herself once again sitting opposite her husband in the living room of their suburban home twelve years in the unchangeable past.

✳ ✳ ✳

Sitting on the couch, Thomas read through the last of the schematics for Pandora. Andrea sat silently in one of the armchairs, thinking. Sunlight filtered through the windows.

"What if I decide to do this? What then?" she asked.

Thomas looked up from the folder. "What do you mean?"

"I mean after we're done, what do we do?"

"We leave," he said Thomas closed the folder, resting it on his lap.

"How?" she asked.

He chuckled. "Sweetheart, you're not making sense."

His smile dissolved as she stood and walked toward the kitchen. "Andrea, I'm not a mind reader. You have to tell me what you're thinking in order for us to have a conversation."

Andrea returned and resumed pacing. "How do we continue living our lives knowing what we know? How are we supposed to keep going through the same routine as if nothing happened? As if we know nothing about what is expected to come?"

Thomas remained silent. She continued to pace. "And what about the past?" she said.

"What about the past?"

Andrea stopped for a moment and looked him in the eyes. "Whether you want to admit it or not, this is going to change us. Probably for the worse. We're going to relive memories both of us have spent our lives trying to forget."

"There aren't any memories I'm afraid to face."

"Really? What about your father's suicide? You're not afraid of reliving that moment? To see his face and know there's nothing you can do to stop him from dying again?"

Thomas sat silently for a moment, his eyes on Andrea, trying not to show the pain of her words, or fear of the possible future. "What about you?" he asked.

"Tom?" Her tone lowered as her face hardened.

"All I'm saying is, it might do us good to talk about this. I don't know anything about your past, and when we agreed to do this—"

"I haven't agreed to anything," Andrea reminded him.

"*If* we agree to do this, it might be beneficial to know what we're getting into. I've told you everything about my past, but you've told me next to nothing about yours"—Thomas hesitated a moment—"not even about how you got those scars on your wrist."

Andrea threw her hands into the air and walked toward the back door. Thomas quickly stood from the couch and raced to his wife, standing in front of her. "Okay. I'll drop it."

He grabbed her hand, pulling her closer. She turned. They both stood face to face, looking at the other, letting their bodies gently touch.

"Listen," he said, "I'm not sure what's going to happen if and when we decide to do this, or how we're going to go back to living our normal lives after it's all said and done. But how are we supposed to get back to living a normal life knowing those folders are on the table? Knowing that somewhere there's a machine built to seed another planet with human life, or that these Clouds and Outages aren't going to go away? Andrea, we have to do this. I don't see how we can't."

She closed her eyes, trying as hard as possible to calm her nerves with little success. Two tears rolled down her cheeks as she shook her head in understanding and acceptance. All Thomas could think to do is pull her close and hold her in his arms. With her head against his chest and his chin resting atop her head, they held onto each other.

"Just promise me one thing. Promise me you'll be there when I need you. Even if I can't tell you everything, just be there. Can you promise me that?"

Andrea's eyes were closed as she listened to her husband's steady heartbeat, letting the tears seep from her eyes as he held her tight and agreed to her request. They were standing there, drawing strength and reinforcement from the other, when the ringing of the telephone broke the stillness. Letting go, and looking at the other with a small smile, Thomas went to the phone beside the couch and lifted the receiver before the third ring. With his eyes on Andrea, he spoke. "Hello?"

"Dr. Charon?" asked the voice.

"Speaking."

"Have you made a decision?"

The smile faded from his face as his eyes shifted to the floor. There was silence on the other end as the caller waited. Thomas looked at Andrea.

"Dr. Charon?" asked the voice again in the same tone.

"Yes, I'm here."

"Have you made a decision?"

Thomas and Andrea looked at each other, realizing what was about to happen, making a silent agreement to continue. "Yes—the answer is yes."

"Both of you?"

"Both of us." Thomas was still looking into Andrea's eyes as she sighed heavily and looked away. A cloud passed overheard, darkening the afternoon sky.

"Good. The two of you will be picked up tomorrow afternoon at 2 p.m. for training on Pandora's operational systems, and further details of the project. From there you'll be transported to the Pandora complex for the completion of your assignment."

"Wait. Tomorrow? We can't leave that soon. We need at least a week to arrange our leave of absence with our departments and offices. We still have classes to teach, grant proposals to finish, and conferences to rearrange. Tomorrow is too—."

"Everything has already been arranged. The car will arrive at 2 p.m. sharp. Don't be late. You are allowed one piece of luggage each. All research materials will be supplied. If you have any further questions, they can be answered upon your arrival. Thank you both for your assistance. We'll see you soon. Goodbye."

When Thomas heard the dial tone, he looked at the phone in confusion before putting the receiver back in its cradle.

"What did he say?" asked Andrea.

"We leave tomorrow."

Before Andrea could respond, time shifted and reality returned.

Four weeks of training—details of all of Pandora rooms, the source of its power, the process of using the IPS, and maneuvering memory replays throughout the computer system—fast-forwarded through their memories, bombarding their brains with so much information that their noses began to bleed.

Breathing hard, Thomas leaned against the computer console and, broke Pandora's connection. Andrea grabbed the sides of her head in an attempt to stifle the pain radiating through her mind. Both were trying to catch their breaths and organize their thoughts. They didn't look at each other.

After standing in silence a few moments, Thomas grabbed the chair at his work station, pulled it to the computer and sat, and began typing. Blood remained on his face. Andrea's hands remained on the side of her head as she stared at the floor.

"I remember," said Andrea.

Thomas kept typing, staring into his monitor as the screens displaying Pandora's progress through the IPS were replaced with window upon window of data. The list of names remained on display. "This wasn't supposed to happen," he said. "They never said this would happen."

Andrea stared absently into space. "It's all been a lie."

"The side effects of Pandora were supposed to be swelling and scarring of the hippocampus, resulting in the loss of time comprehension, losing one's mind, and an inability to return to the present."

"How could I have been so stupid?" Andrea asked herself, not moving.

"They never said anything about a complete loss of memory and its slow progression of returning through shared flashes, filling in the gaps left by the machine. Something is different. This wasn't supposed to happen," Thomas continued.

He continued to type, bringing up window after window of Pandora's schematics. Andrea dropped her hands and looked at Thomas. "You lied to me."

Thomas continued to type, oblivious to everything but the keyboard.

"You *lied* to me," she said, louder.

"What?"

"You promised you'd be there for me when the replays began, but you weren't."

Thomas stopped typing and turned to Andrea. He said nothing, just stared absently into Andrea's expressionless face, unsure of what she meant. Before he could speak, his mind was transported back to when they first entered the Pandora complex.

✳ ✳ ✳

With the doors closed and the hatch locked, the generators running and the complex fully lit, Thomas and Andrea stood on the white tiled floor in the hall of Pandora for the first time, staring into the unchanging eyes of the man in the black suit—Munin.

"Before you begin, there's one final detail that we must still discuss. As you know, the number of clouds around the globe are too numerous to count—and they seem to be moving closer to one another. Luckily, Pandora is protected from Outages by the EMP bubble created by the four large generators in a room beneath this facility. Although we remain optimistic that atmospheric circumstances will improve, and Project Pandora wouldn't need to be launched, we also know that atmospheric conditions could get out of control in the years to come. If this occurs, and it becomes evident that conditions are too severe to manage, we will call upon the both of you to return."

They looked at Munin, confused. "Return?" asked Thomas. "To do what?"

"To continue work on Pandora."

"What? That wasn't part of the agreement," said Andrea.

Munin's face did not change. "The agreement has changed."

"You can't do that!" yelled Andrea angrily. Thomas reached out to calm her. She knocked his hand away and took a step closer to Munin. He did not move.

"Andrea . . ."

"We've gone through the training, put our lives on hold, and now you're telling us the agreement has *changed*?"

"I'm sorry, Dr. Charon, but what life do you think you'll be returning to if this project fails?"

"The same as if it succeeds," Andrea responded without hesitation.

The hall went silent as the tension eased. There were no apologies—just more questions. "How long will this agreement last?" asked Thomas.

"As long as it must."

"Or as long as we survive?" Andrea put her hands on her hips, inches from Munin.

"What would happen if we refuse?" Thomas asked.

"It would be viewed as a breach of contract, and a waste of government time, resources, and training. There would be repercussions."

"Being—"

"Seven to fifteen years in federal prison, $150,000 fine . . . each, and—"

Andrea stopped pacing. "What the hell is your problem?" She stood in front of Thomas and stared Munin in the eyes. He did not look away. The question remained in the air, unanswered.

"Do you agree to the new terms or not, Mrs. Charon?"

Andrea held his gaze and answered. "Yes."

Munin turned to Thomas. "And what about you, Dr. Charon?"

Thomas hesitated. With fists clenched at his side and his eyes on the floor, he nodded.

Without affirming that they understood the new terms of the agreement, Munin began explaining the final instructions. "The planet you are targeting is Gliese. All the materials you'll need, when not working directly with Pandora, will be in the research room. When you've completed the assignment—calculating the route to Gliese by the use of the IPS and sorting the loaded memories in the databanks—Pandora will shut itself down, at which time a signal for us to return will be transmitted. After we receive the signal, a helicopter will return to this location and retrieve you in no more than three hours. Afterward, you will return to the training facility for a follow-up report, physical, and payment for your services. However, I am to advise you that if either of you are in danger of losing your life, a code can be entered that will unlock the hatch and allow an emergency exit and shut down Pandora. When the code is loaded, Pandora will shut itself down and retrieval procedures will commence. If you enter the code when there's no emergency, you will suffer the repercussions I already mentioned.

"In essence, the code I'm about to give you is only to be used in absolutely dire circumstances. *Only* use it when there are no other possible solutions. Is that understood?"

They nodded.

"The code is 53843. You can also remember it as the word 'Lethe.'"

"Lethe?" asked Andrea. "Like the River of Forgetfulness."

"Yes. Are there any other questions?" Neither spoke. "If there are none, I will leave. Good luck to the both of you. And we look forward to hearing from you soon."

Without another word, Munin walked to the ladder, entered the security code, lifted the hatch, and exited. Andrea and Thomas watched as the lid closed, locking them within the walls of their own past. They stood and waited, not sure for what.

Thomas allowed his hands to relax and anger to subside. Andrea said and did nothing, only continued to stare at the metallic hatch, white walls, and silver handles. He turned to her. "Well, should we get started?"

Without replying, Andrea followed Thomas to Pandora's control room and entered. There they found black screens, blank monitors, and an array of buttons. Thomas looked to the switch in the center of the console he'd been told would power up the computer. , Andrea met his gaze, knowing what was to come. With a small smile and quick exhale, he stepped to the computer control panel, lifted the green cover, and flipped the switch from off to on, bringing with it the whir of cooling fans.

One by one lights appeared under green and red buttons, reports moved from screen to screen on both monitors, and images waited to be brought up on the screens. Andrea and Thomas watched as if life were being created before their eyes, expecting visions of their past to immediately appear. All that waited before them were untouched keyboards ready to be put to use. They looked at each other, then, without speaking, went to their work stations, pulled out their chairs, cleared their minds, and got to work.

As the hours progressed, they worked in silence, unsure of what to say, apprehensive of what was to come. After searching through the databanks, making notes of all the charts, graphs, details of the software, and tasks that would soon await him, Thomas stared at his computer screen, absent of thought, waiting for the first of the copied memories to appear on his monitor. Andrea also stared into her monitor, making calculations and charting the future course of Pandora as the screens to the front of the room displayed its gravitational movements. Thomas was unsure of what next to do when pain suddenly shot through his legs and shins, as if he were running along sidewalks and through open fields. Before he could groan, the pain vanished. When he looked back to the computer screen, he saw the first of the memories was uploaded and waiting.

He said nothing to Andrea. He just started to work, studying the copied memory labeled *Physical Endurance*, taken from his own thoughts.

Pandora did not read the visual images or emotions of the memory, only the categories in which could be classified: physical endurance, stamina, shin pain, burning, and muscle strength. Looking through the many sections, categories, and subcategories, Thomas wondered how he and Andrea could ever fill that many sections without losing their minds. The question plagued him for the remainder of the day.

That night, Andrea lay in bed beside the sleeping Thomas when the smell of dust and wood filled the room, reminding her of the scent of the attic in her childhood home and vanishing as quickly as it manifested. Believing it to be a figment of her imagination, she closed her eyes when she heard the faint sound of Sirens approaching. She opened her eyes and sat up—and the sound vanished. Thomas did not stir. Not knowing what to make of it, she stared into the blackness of the room. The only sound was the distant hum of electricity. Andrea lay back, closed her eyes, and tried to sleep.

After a few hours of restless sleep, both were awake, feeling slightly refreshed. That morning, for reasons Thomas could not explain, feelings of sadness washed over him as he showered. As the fifteen-minute allotment was up, those feelings were replaced by happy ones of childhood afternoons spent with his father.

Andrea, meanwhile, experienced a range of emotions as she dressed, from depression to excitement.

As they prepared to enter the control room, fear of what lay on the other side overcame them. As Thomas reached for the door, both were on the verge of tears, laughter, and panic, but all these emotions quickly dissolved. Entering, they sat and began to work. Neither told the other what had occurred.

More memories waited to be sorted.

Throughout the day, neither spoke. They sat in the kitchen during one of their breaks and stared into their coffee cups. In the black liquid were the constellations of Orion, Cepheus, Antila, locations of spiraling galaxies and nebulas Andrea would never see in person but knew existed. Unable to blink, mesmerized by the beauty of the darkened vacuum, she scanned the sky from left to right, noting the placement of stars, smelling the night air, and feeling comfort course through her body with the cool autumn breeze. Turning her head from the night sky, she looked back down into her coffee.

Thomas watched the creamer swirl in the coffee in his cup. Before his hands could move toward the spoon on the table, his child-sized fingers turned the page to reveal new images of caped heroes and balloons filled with words, bringing excitement and joy in a black-and-white, no matter how colorful the pages. Before he could finish reading the first page, the heroes and villains disappeared, replaced by the contents of his cup.

They looked across the table at each other, both realizing it was the beginning.

"That was when you lied," Andrea said. The kitchen and coffee of the past were replaced by the control room, work stations, and monitors of Pandora of the present.

"What?"

"When that pain shot up your leg, you should have told me."

"Told you what?"

"That it started."

"That it started? What was I supposed to say?"

"Anything. Something."

"And what about you?" Thomas said.

"What about me?"

"You didn't say anything either."

Andrea opened the door of the control room, wiped the blood from her face, and walked down the hall toward her room. Thomas followed.

Andrea turned in the center of the hall to face Thomas. "You promised. You promised to be there. Before we agreed to this project you promised to help. Instead you did nothing, forcing me to relive each memory alone. Again."

Andrea turned to walk away, but she was stopped by the scent of sweat, wood, and the sensation of bare skin in the cool night air as their minds traveled twelve years in the past to the first vivid memories of themselves in the walls of Pandora.

✳ ✳ ✳

"Tom? What are you doing?"

The sound of Andrea's voice pulled Thomas from darkness to blinding light. Confused and disoriented, he opened his eyes to find Pandora's white walls millimeters from his face as he stood in the far corner of the room he and Andrea shared.

The muscles in his legs were like Jell-O weak, unable to support weight. Emotions of sadness, loneliness, and depression prevailed as he turned from the corner to his wife's confused, fear-stricken face. Tears rolled down his cheeks, and he didn't know why.

Standing only in his boxers and white socks, Thomas looked from one side of the room to the other, bewildered. Andrea sat on the bed, staring at her husband, unsure of what to say or do. Both knew what had just taken place.

"It happened?" she asked.

Thomas said nothing. He stood still, trying to let the sadness drain from his body to the floor. But they remained, making him feel as if he was waking from a nightmare that was now his total existence.

"You had a Replay, didn't you," she said.

He walked slowly to the bed and sat on the edge. Andrea sat in the middle, staring at her husband's bare back and short hair. Thomas's gaze remained steady on the handle and gray exterior of the door, attempting to make sense of the thoughts, feelings, and emotions, battling one another throughout his mind and body. He reached up, wiped the remnants of a tear from his right cheek, and placed his hand back to his lap.

"I can still smell pine, oak." He spoke slowly, trying to make sense of his words. "The muscles in my legs feel like they'll seize at any minute. I feel the bottoms of my feet where the blisters were after that night. The fear, the pain, every emotion I had on that day is pulsating through my body. I know where I am, I know what happened, but it all felt so real. Like it just happened, and there was nothing I could do to stop it."

Andrea sat silently, listening, unsure of how to react.

Minutes passed. Neither moved or spoke.

Stiff from exhaustion, gravity took over, and Thomas lowered his head to the pillow. Stretching out, he kept his eyes focused directly ahead. Andrea stared at his defined profile and open eyes, not wanting to move. After a few moments, she lay down.

Neither closed their eyes as motion-sensitive lights flickered out twelve years in the past before coming on twelve years in the future, their minds returning to the fully lit hall of Pandora in the present.

Dazed from the sudden bombardment of foreboding memories, Andrea placed her hand on the wall, steadying her body and anchoring her thoughts. Two drops of blood dripped from her nose to the floor.

A dull pain radiated in Thomas's head as he stared at the outline of her middle-aged face. "That night, the memory I had was of the day I celebrated my graduation from high school and the death of my father." Andrea stared into the wall. Thomas continued to speak. "After the motorcycle accident, he had blinding headaches and pain in his amputated leg whenever there was an Outage. I remember him saying a few days before he died that the headaches felt like tectonic plates grinding against one another inside his skull. For two years he suffered that pain, going from doctor to doctor, none able to explain why it was happening. It was just another mystery created by the Clouds that was swept under the rug as unexplainable. My mom and I tried to help him through it as best we could, but there was only so much we could do. Eventually, it . . ."

Tears welled in Thomas's eyes as he suffered the thoughts of his father's agony. He continued as water and blood mingled on white tiles. "When I found him on the floor of the bathroom, my mind went blank. The shock and pain of what happened made me shut down. I didn't know what to do, I didn't know what to think, so my body took over. With my clothes and hands stained by my father's blood, I walked through the crowd of family and friends. I couldn't see their faces, or hear their voices. To me they were only blurs and shadows. The only thing that mattered was the street. I had to get out.

"I ran through abandoned roads, dying parks, and silent houses. I ran until it felt as if my heart were going to burst from my chest. With each step I wanted to rip some part of me out and beat it to the ground. I wanted the pain in my legs, lungs, and chest to match the pain I felt for my father, or the rage at the Cloud hovering above."

Sadness became anger, and Andrea listened. "The world was silent, peaceful, calm, and I hated it. With each step I stripped off the clothes with my dad's blood. When my clothing was gone, and all I had left were boxers and socks, I screamed as hard as I could. I wanted to shake the Clouds from the sky, let them know and feel my anger, to strike me down where I stood, to do anything. But they did nothing. They remained silent, blanketing the sky in darkness, and flashing silent white light. Nothing changed. The Clouds, my sadness, anger, fear, everything remained just as it was. The only difference after hours of running, besides a sore throat and aching muscles, was that I felt more alone and hollow than I had in my entire life. I didn't know what to do, so I did nothing. I went home and did nothing as I waited for it to pass. I'm still waiting."

Thomas stared at the floor, dried tears on his cheeks. He looked up into Andrea's eyes before continuing. "Is that what you wanted to hear? Because if it is, why didn't you ask? Why didn't *you* say anything? Why didn't *you* try and help that night? You're not the only one who went through this alone."

Her eyes on Thomas, she spoke calmly, without emotion. "I did try to help."

Wrinkles receded, blood vanished from white tiles, but Pandora's walls, rooms, and hall remained unchanged. Thomas and Andrea Charon sat across from one another, each with a cup of coffee at the kitchen table, twelve years in the past.

✳ ✳ ✳

They sat across from one another in Pandora's kitchen. Andrea was staring into his exhausted face as he leaned forward, his elbows resting on the table. He kept his eyes focused on his cup of coffee. He hadn't slept.

"Tom, talk to me. Tell me what happened."

Silent, Thomas continued to stare absently into his cup."

She leaned forward in an attempt to get his attention. "How long were you out?"

"The only thing I remember is seeing you standing in the corner of the room, staring into the wall."

The black liquid was still in Thomas's cup, cooling, holding his attention.

"Did it have something to do with your father?"

When he didn't respond, Andrea heaved a heavy sigh, sat up, and rested her back against the chair. Thomas did not move. She searched his face for answers, but found none. Frustrated, she stood from the table and walked to the door of the kitchen.

"I'll be in the research room. Come get me when you're ready to work." Without looking back, she walked out the door and into the hall.

Andrea sat at the table in the center of the research room and began absentmindedly looking through her notes. Pages shook in her hands—not because of the daunting task of calculating a course from this solar system to the next (using the trajectory and velocity of other planets and asteroids to ensure the surviving memory of her race) but because she would have to relive aspects of her past that were meant to remain buried.

Andrea stared at the words, equations, maps, and outlines, but her mind focused on Thomas's absent expression the night before, his complete failure to understand which time period he was in, and why he wouldn't answer her questions. And she had so many. What happened? Where did he go? What did he see? Did it all happen in the same sequence as previously, or did it jump from one memory before splicing into another?

Details of Pandora's schematic, explaining how the re-plays would begin gradual before becoming more vivid, made her question whether or not to believe it was true.

As her thoughts raced from one to the other, a low mur-mur began to fill the room. Andrea put down her notebook and looked around. All she saw were books, rolled maps, and loose-leaf sheets as the sound continued to build.

It was the jumbled, unintelligible words and laughter of students she was hearing. One voice stood out above the oth-ers. At first few words and phrases were recognizable, but she soon could understand more. Trying to pick words out of the jumbled murmur, she realized the words on the pages were blurring as Professor Jonathan Loki came into focus opposite her in a booth in the dining hall, staring at Andrea with an awkward smile.

Andrea's half-empty glass of water sat on the table be-tween them, untouched. She stared at her hands on the table, noting the contrast between her skin and the wood finish. Jonathan's words stumbled over themselves. "Do you come here often?" He realized how absurd his words sounded as they left his lips.

"Umm . . . this is my first time. I know some of the profes-sors have lunch with their students, sometimes, but I never really saw the point. I heard the food was okay, but . . . I guess . . ."

He sat looked around the cafeteria. "God, what am I do-ing! What are you doing?" he asked. He leaned across the table, his voice lower. "I'm married. You're a student. How old are you anyway? Twenty-one? Twenty-two?" Andrea said nothing, keeping her eyes on the table and head down. "I'm happily married," he said. "I shouldn't have done this. Why did I do this? My God, what have I done?"

He rubbed his temples and closed his eyes. Andrea's ex-pression had not changed. She refused to look across the table at her professor's face and the reality of their situation. He leaned against the table and looked around the room, feeling more frustrated and lost.

"Why did you . . ." he began, then lowered his voice and leaned forward again. "Why did you kiss me? What were you thinking? This could destroy my career. You know that, right?" Andrea said nothing.

"Do you want something? Admission into the graduate program? Money? A guaranteed A in the class? What?"

Still she said nothing, making him more frustrated and angry. "Well?" he asked. "*Say* something."

Andrea glared down. Jonathan looked across the table, staring into her face. The conversations and laughter of other students slowed time to a halt.

Unable to take Andrea's silence, Jonathan stood from the table. "All I want . . ." she began as he rose. "All I want is to see you again. I won't tell if you won't."

He looked down at her. Unsure of what to do, he said. "I have to go."

He walked toward the exit. She didn't follow him, neither with her eyes or her feet, but she knew it would happen again. Her attention remained on the blank white wall of the Pandora research room as it settled into silence, causing the booth, Professor Loki, and the murmur of college students to vanish into the past, as if they never existed.

She blinked, looking from one side of the room to the other before gazing into Thomas's eyes as he stood in the open doorway.

"Did you hear me?"

"What?" she asked in a daze.

Both their faces and voices were a wash of emotion and color. "I asked if you were ready to get back to work."

"Oh . . . yeah," she said, searching her thoughts for the correct response. "I'll be right there. I just have to finish this calculation."

Her eyes drifted to the pages on the table. Thomas hesitated, unsure of what to say, but not wanting to start another argument. Instead he closed the door, leaving Andrea to herself and severing the connection to Pandora twelve years in the past and the Pandora twelve years in the future, copying, and replaying stored memories.

Thomas and Andrea sat on the floor in the hall. Blood ran from their noses to their chins, adding more stains from their tattered past. He looked at her. "Who was that?" he said. She wiped the blood from her face, but didn't try to stand. "What was he talking about?"

She said nothing. Staring at him, she could see the anger behind his eyes and his hardened expression. She sat silently, unmoving, before trying to stand. She leaned against the wall for support. "Nothing," she said.

Thomas remained on the floor, looking up. "It didn't seem like nothing."

"Tom, drop it."

He began to smile, then laughed softly. She looked down at him in surprise, as he kept on chuckling, wiping blood from his face with his sleeve. "What's so funny?" she asked.

He didn't answer right away. He continued to laugh as he stood and looked into her eyes. "You were having an affair."

Both stood facing each other, Thomas smiling as Andrea's face became expressionless. She turned and entered the research room. and Thomas followed.

"How long did it last?" he asked.

"I don't want to talk about it."

"You really need to find better ways of avoiding conversations."

Andrea circled to the other side of the table and sat, avoiding eye contact. He stood, staring, no longer smiling, bombarding her with question after inappropriate question. "How did it start? How many times did you have sex? How many kids did he have? Who broke it off—you or him? Did it hurt? Do you still think of him? What is he doing now? Where he is? Is he the reason you slit your wrists?"

She remained silent, head down, studying the notes spread on the table. He stood over her, hands planted in the center of the table, restricting her view and staring into her face.

"Do you know what really makes me upset?" he said. "Not the fact that you were having an affair with a married man, or the fact that you never told me about it, but the fact that *you* lied, not *me*."

Andrea looked into his eyes. She still said nothing.

"You weren't there for me that morning, or that night. You've never been there for me—not like I've been there for you. Those questions you were asking had nothing to do with me. You wanted to know about my replay so *you* knew what to expect, not to make sure I was okay. I've been patient, kind, understanding, and all you've been to me is cold, hurtful, and dishonest. You said the reason you had problems after sex was because of what happened to you as a kid. I didn't press the issue because I thought, idiot that I was, that you would tell me in your own time, when you were ready. Now I find you lied so I would stop asking questions, shut up, and see you as the victim. Because you had no problem sleeping with a married man twice your age while still in college."

Tears began to form in Andrea's eyes.

"Am I right?" he asked. She said nothing.

"Well, it worked. I didn't press the issue then, and rest assured I'm not going to press the issue now. I'm still the same pushover I've always been. Just know now that you're alone because you want to be. Your fear, loneliness, and depression is because of you, not me, or anyone else. I tried to get through to you, and all you had to do was tell the truth. Instead you constantly bit my head off and told me nothing. Now that I know, you can keep your secrets. I'm done."

Thomas turned and walked away. As he reached for the door handle, tears fell from Andrea's eyes, allowing both of them to feel the fresh linen beneath Andrea's body, and the gauze around her wrists as both were transported to the bed of a hospital in Andrea's past.

✳ ✳ ✳

The room was calm, dark. Outside, voices were murmuring. Shadows passed beneath the door. The only light came from a dim lamp on the headboard, illuminating a portion of the room. The rest faded into darkness. As her eyes wandered from left to right, her blurred vision sharpened somewhat.

The smell of antiseptic permeated the room. Through the dim haze she saw white walls with framed landscapes above smooth tiled floors. In the corner was a sink, cabinets, and darkened television mounted to the wall. To the right were large windows, the blinds open to reveal a clear night sky and full moon, creating elongated shadows.

The constellations and lunar craters brought back memories, reminding Andrea of the tree house, the steel blade, and pain. Her mind and heart raced. Sensations of cold steel and warm blood running down her wrist to the floor returned, causing pain and panic to radiate through her head from the sudden rush of blood.

Restraints binding Andrea's wrists to the sides of the bed kept her from rubbing her temples. Moving caused pain and the leather straps to tighten around the white gauze on her wrists.

"Try not to struggle. You'll only worsen the wounds and make them reopen. They need time to heal." Andrea looked left to see her mother sitting in the chair beside her head.

"They said it was a precaution they take with all attempted suicides. It's to ensure you don't harm yourself any more than you already have."

Andrea tried to move her legs and found they were bound as well. She stared at her arms, legs, the restraints, and the cotton gown covering her body.

"Are you thirsty?" Evelyn Remus Tyr reached for a glass of water on the night stand and turned to her daughter. "The doctor said since you lost so much blood from the . . . accident, you'd wake up feeling dizzy."

Evelyn placed the glass to Andrea's lips, which remained clamped shut.

Heaving a sigh of frustration, but saying nothing, Evelyn placed the glass back on the nightstand. She moved her hand toward Andrea's head, but then pulled it back. "After I found you in that tree house, I didn't know what to do. You were lying there on the floor—and there was so much blood. I still don't know how I got you out and back to the house. Luckily, Daryl was there."

At the mention of his name, Andrea turned toward her mother and looked into her eyes.

"Is that were you've been going all this time?" Evelyn asked. "I saw all the books, your magazines, the telescope, binoculars. It all was there. Did you move your stuff out there after Michael died?"

Breaking eye contact, Andrea looked at the restraint binding her right wrist and pulled with all her might, causing the bed to shake.

"Andrea, stop—you're going to hurt yourself." Evelyn placed her hand on Andrea's shoulder. Andrea pulled away.

"I don't care," she said in an angry whisper. With more force, she pulled and kicked both her arms and legs, knocking away Evelyn's hand.

"Andrea—*stop*!"

"I don't *care*," she said, louder this time.

Blood seeped through the gauze around her wrists as Evelyn tried to hold her down and restrict her movements. Screams filled the air as pain radiated from Andrea's mind to Thomas's wrists, inches from the research room door. Tears streamed down the sides of her face, mixing with the blood running from her nose.

Thomas stared at the door's smooth metallic finish. He placed his hand on the handle. "I was raped," she said softly to his back. He paused but didn't turn around.

She didn't stand. Pink-stained star maps were spread on the table. " My mom worked nights. Mike, my brother, was there to watch me most nights, but when he . . . died, there was no one. Then Daryl came, and, when my mom was gone he would . . ." Tears continued to fall.

"He was my step-father, Tom. That's why I slit my wrists. Not because of John, but because I couldn't take it anymore. Daryl paid most of the bills and knew if I said anything my mom would lose her job and he would leave. We would have been out on the street. I didn't know what else to do. Everything was just too hard, and . . ."

She was overtaken by sobs, preventing her from continuing. Thomas stood expressionless and silent. Her eyes shifted to the table, watching as tears and blood mixed on its surface, letting the emotions from her past take over.

"And what?" he said, still facing the closed door. His hand remained on the handle.

Andrea stared, unbelievingly. "What . . .?" Tears continued to fall. "What do you want me to say?"

"Nothing, Andrea. I don't want you to say anything."

Thomas opened the door, and went out into the hall. He took two steps, then dropped to the floor.

Tears fell as he listened to Andrea sob through the door.

Warmth spread through his body. The sensation of dripping sweat and exhausted muscles invaded his senses as lights overhead dimmed to darkness. The smell of lavender filled the halls of his childhood home as he entered the open foyer, exhausted from another night of running under white lightning and black Clouds.

❋ ❋ ❋

The sound of the closing door echoed in the dark foyer. Thomas, exhausted, was dripping sweat as he entered, his footsteps ricocheting off the hardwood floor partly covered by a large, flowery throw rug. He walked toward the stairs leading up to his room.

A light appeared, and to the left he saw Laura Charon silhouetted in the light of the lamp on the table beside her chair. They stared through the open doorway at each other. Neither was smiling.

"We need to . . ." she started.

Without allowing her to finish, he turned from the stairs to the hall toward the kitchen, turning on lights as he went. Laura stood and followed.

"Tom."

They entered the kitchen. Thomas went to the sink, took a glass from the cupboard, and filled it with water. Laura stood in front of the kitchen table, arms at her side, staring at her son's sweat-soaked back.

"You can't keep doing this. You can't spend your days locked inside this house and nights running the streets. Do you know how dangerous these storms can be?"

Thomas leaned against the counter top, drinking the contents of his glass before placing it into the stainless steel sink. Walking past his mother through the hall back toward the foyer, he said nothing as he climbed the stairs to his room.

Laura followed. "Talk to me, Tom—please. Since you father passed, you've said next to nothing. I know it's hard, but you have to talk to me. And we still have to discuss settling your father's estate before you go off to college in a few months."

"I'm not going," was his only response as he continued toward his room. His voice was monotone, emotionless.

She paused for a moment before continuing up the steps. "What?" she asked, not sure she'd heard him correctly.

"I said I'm not going. And you can settle Dad's estate on your own. I don't want the money he left me and I don't care what you do with it."

Thomas turned at the top of the stairs, walked past the bathroom where his father's dead body had lain a few months earlier, and went to his room. Before Laura could respond, he went in closed the door behind him, leaving his mother standing there, staring at it. It took her a moment to gather her senses before reopening the door and entering.

He stood at the corner of his desk near his computer, wiping the sweat from his wet body with a towel. The floor, desk, and bed were covered with clothes and books of fiction, biography, web design, autobiography, software development, and nonfiction science.

"What do you mean, you're not going to college?" Thomas continued wiping sweat from his body. "Tom, you have to go to college."

"No I don't," he said without looking at her.

"Yes you do. What you do with the money your father left you is your business. If you don't want to help me with the estate, that's fine. I can understand. I can't tell you how to spend the money, but the choice of whether or not you go to college is not up to you. You may think it is, but it's not. You might be eighteen, but you're still my son and you have too much potential to skip college. You've won scholarships, enrolled in classes, made housing arrangements—everything. You *have* to go."

Thomas stripped off his wet shirt and threw it into the hamper on the other side of the room, then picked up another from the chair beside his desk and pulled it on. He looked at the books scattered on his desk before pushing the power button on his computer. "No—I *don't*," he repeated.

"Is this because of me?" He looked at his mother. "Are you afraid to leave me here alone?" she asked. "Because if you are, don't be. I'll be fine."

Thomas's eyes softened, but his features remained stiff. "No, Mom—it's not you."

"Then what is it?" She stared into her son's eyes, searching for clues to emotions hidden beneath layers of anger, confusion, depression, and loneliness. She found none.

"You sit around the house all day . . ."

He walked past his mother out the door and back toward the stairs. She continued to speak as she followed. "You don't say anything, you don't talk to anyone."

Thomas walked down the steps. "You won't answer the phone. I can't tell you how many times I've had to lie to Mel when she called, or when she knocked on the door. She thinks you've already gone to school. Do you know how hurt she was that you never said goodbye? All you do is sit in your room and work on your computer or read."

Thomas walked from the stairs back to the kitchen. "When you're not reading, you're running." Thomas walked through the kitchen to the door leading to the attached garage. "And when you're not running you're working on . . . *this*."

When Thomas opened the door, the scent of lavender gave way to the stale smell of axle grease and motor oil. Thomas turned on the light to reveal the cause of his father's missing leg and eventual death—a partially reconstructed motorcycle. Strewn on the oil-stained cement floor were nuts, bolts, screws, and parts that all needed to go back into the frame. Screwdrivers, wrenches, hammers—tools of all shapes, sizes, and functions—were scattered on the work-benches along the wall.

Without speaking or turning to look at his mother, Thomas went to the stool in front of the motorcycle, picked up a socket wrench, and started to work.

Laura stood in the doorway, angry, refusing to enter. "Why do you do this? Why do you keep working on that . . . thing? That motorcycle took your father's leg and ruined his life. It killed him, Tom! Like you, he spent hours locked in his room. Only he was crying out in pain from headaches. When he wasn't upstairs, he was down here working on this bike. Now you're doing the same thing. It's idiotic!"

"It was *his!*" Thomas yelled. Thomas stood and stared at his mother, his voice stunning her into silence. "It was what he loved. It was what he loved to do, and it's all I have left of him! You think I don't know it's stupid? You think I don't try and talk myself out of working on this . . . thing?"

He turned and threw the socket wrench at the bike before turning back to his mother. "Well, I do. I know what I need to do. I know what's logical, intelligent. I know I need to go to college, talk to Mel, not go out during the Outages, or spend the entire day locked in my room. But it's all I can do. It's all I know how to do. If I don't work on this bike, or run, or read, or do something to keep my mind occupied, I'll break down. Is that what you want to hear, Mom? Because if it is, then I've said it and all I want you to do is stop, please, and give me some time to figure this out. I don't know why, and I don't know for how long, but I know it's what I need—at least for now. So please, just . . . just—"

He couldn't finish. He didn't need to. There were no tears in his eyes. His hands shook with anger. All Laura could do was stand silently and accept her son's explanation.

Without speaking, she stepped back into the kitchen, leaving Thomas alone in the garage. He watched as she closed the door and listened as her muffled footsteps faded, his immediate world settling into silence. Physically drained and mentally exhausted, he returned to the motorcycle, picked up the socket wrench, and stared at the wreck.

Sitting alone where he once looked on as his father worked on his prized possession, all Thomas could do was stare absently into the scrapes and dents from the accident that claimed his father's leg. Unable to move, he felt the delayed impact of his words and the emotions that had remained dormant since the death of his father reverberated through his mind with the sound of the single gunshot. The purple and orange paintwork on the bike's frame blurred as tears came to his eyes. Words of anger and confusion were replaced with sobs of grief as the socket wrench fell from his hand to the floor.

The smell of motor oil was replaced by the scent of blood, the parts on the floor became smooth white tiles. Thomas sat on the floor as Pandora's white walls came into view and mourned the loss of his father for the second time in his life.

The handle of the research room door turned silently and swung open slowly on its hinges. Andrea stepped into the hall, leaving the door open, and stood between Thomas's spread legs as he sat on the floor, his back against the wall, his head in his hands.

Both their shirts, sleeves, and faces were streaked with blood. Andrea looked down on Thomas' still body, face still wet with tears. Neither moved, but both knew something needed to be said. Keeping her eyes on Thomas, Andrea sat against the opposite wall.

"What are we doing?" Thomas asked, his head still in hands. "Why are we even here? What's the point?"

Before Andrea could respond, the tiles gradually darkened from white to blue, finally settling as the brown and black of wooden floorboards. The sterile, ventilated air became thick with unsettled dust. Sunlight radiated through a closed window as Andrea's middle-aged eyes regained the clarity of a child. She was looking through the contents of an open blue trunk on the attic floor of her childhood home. Boxes of outdated clothing and outgrown shoes with worn soles collected dust along the creaking attic floorboards.

"Anne? You up here?" a voice called from the stairs.

Andrea turned to see Michael's head, as he climbed the steps leading to the upper level of the house. Looking to his right, he locked eyes with his younger sister. "What are you doing up here?" he asked. He walked up the remaining steps and approached his sister.

"What's this?" she asked.

"What's what?" He knelt beside her and looked in the trunk. He saw a disassembled black telescope and a tattered book with the faded image of man on the back of a winged horse.

"This?." A smile appeared on his face. "This is a telescope. You take this"—he took the eyepiece from the trunk and held it to his right eye, closing the other. "Look through this. And when you connect all the pieces together you can use it to look at the stars and planets."

"Who's was it?" she asked.

Michael took the piece from his eye. " Dad's."

"This was Dad's?" she asked with wonder as excitement radiated in her voice.

Michael nodded. "I remember seeing him bent over this telescope staring at the night sky, or sitting on the couch reading this book." He picked up the tattered book and flipped through its pages.

"What is it?"

"This, sweet sister of mine, is the complete origin of our family history."

Andrea's young eyes looked up at her brother, puzzled.

"What?" he asked in mock confusion. "Don't tell me you don't know?"

Andrea shook her head. Michael grabbed his head in exaggerated shock.

"What? Told me what?" Andrea asked, excited.

"I can't believe no one told you. I thought for sure you would have figured it out when you discovered superhuman strength, x-ray vision, or lightening speed."

"What are you talking about?"

"You really don't know?" he asked, sensing the growing annoyance in her voice.

"Come on, Mike—just tell me!"

Andrea grabbed her brother's sleeve, pleading for information. Michael smiled. "Well, if you really must know, even though I'm sure you'd have figured it out on your own. We're . . ." He paused. "Are you sure no one told you?"

"*Mike!*"

"We're gods, okay? We're gods."

Andrea looked at Michael, surprised, shocked, and confused. "What do you mean gods? Like God?"

A look of mock disgust washed over Michael's face. "What are they teaching in school these days? I'm talking about Greek and Roman gods." Andrea still looked confused. He continued. "Hercules, Jupiter, Mars, Venus."

"Those aren't gods. Those are planets." Andrea said, at a loss.

"What do you mean, they aren't gods?" he asked. "The planets were named after us. I guess the next thing you're going to say is you don't know where our last name comes from." Andrea looked at Michael with confusion.

"You don't know where our last name comes from?" She shook her head. "Wow! You really have been deprived."

Michael took the mythology book and sat on the couch. Andrea snuggled up to him as he turned to the page displaying the image of a female wolf and two boys.

"Well, according to legend, we are the descendants of Mars, the god of war. From what Dad told me, Romulus and his twin brother, Remus, were the founders of an ancient city that grew to be one of the strongest to ever to exist. When the boys were born, they were in danger of being killed by their evil uncle, who feared that one day they might try to kill him and take his money and power. To save their lives, they were placed in a basket and sent downriver. After a few days of drifting down waters filled with deadly alligators and crocodiles, the basket was found by a female wolf when it floated ashore."

Thomas pointed to the image of the wolf finding the twin boys in the basket.

"Did she try and eat them?" Andrea asked, nestling closer to her brother, afraid the story was about to take a gruesome turn for the worse.

"No. She did just the opposite—she helped them. She let the boys drink her milk to make sure they didn't die."

"That's gross."

Thomas smiled. "Yeah, a little. After the boys had grown they were found by a shepherd, who took them into his home and raised them as his sons. When they grew up, they decided to create their own city where the wolf found them. They built its foundations, named it Rome, and gave the people the power to make laws. It was the first of its kind. When they died, they joined the gods and became part of the stars and constellations we see at night. Now do you understand who we were?" Michael asked.

A smile spread across Andrea's face. "We were gods!"

Sunlight vanished, dust dissolved, Thomas reappeared, and the white walls of Pandora replaced the cobwebs and wooden walls of an ancient attic filled with boxes and a beaten sofa. Both sat on opposite sides of the hall with fresh blood streaming from their noses to the tips of their chins.

Thomas looked into Andrea's eyes and exhausted face which held a small, but prevalent smile. "That's why you read mythology."

"Actually, he was wrong," she said, looking at him.

"About what?"

"Everything. Romulus and Remus didn't build Rome. Romulus finished building Rome after killing Remus with a shovel in an argument over who the gods favored as king."

"Oh," he said, shocked.

Andrea chuckled softly before continuing. "But I didn't find that out until much later. Either way it wouldn't have mattered. After we put together the telescope, I never left the attic. I studied the stars, read books on mythology, researched different myths and their connections to the constellations, read scientific magazines and journals, and memorized monthly sky charts and almanacs. It got to the point where Mike had to carry me to bed most nights because I'd fallen asleep on the couch in the attic waiting for an eclipse or meteor shower."

Again she laughed to herself. Thomas smiled and listened as she stared off into space, still visiting pleasant memories of her past. "Some nights, when he would come home late after being out with his friends, he would come to the attic and we would watch the stars together. I never told my mom when he left me home alone, and he never told her when I stayed up past curfew. It was our agreement. We looked out for each other."

Her voice trailed as the smile and laughter began to fade. Thomas continued to listen. "Everything made sense. Everything was simple. But after he died, all that changed. The only things that made sense were constellations, myths, and—"

"The hope that one day, when you wake up, things would be better," Thomas continued, "but they never were. The pain stayed, depression lingered, and thoughts of suicide trailed one another until it became the only consistency in the nightmare of reality."

Shocked, Andrea looked up from the tiled floor to Thomas as the face of a young woman quickly flashed before her eyes. Before the image could vanish, Andrea saw the girl's smile. Her hair was long, brown, straight, and her skin was full of color.

Thomas continued. "So to keep the demons at bay, you keep moving. You learn, read, do research—anything and everything to keep from thinking about them."

Andrea saw the girl again, but she'd changed. The smile had stiffened to a tight-lipped grin, her hair had thinned and her skin faded, and her eyes looked as if their color had been washed away. Before the image could vanish again, she sensed she knew this girl, but wasn't sure how. Tears began to form along the rims of Thomas's eyes.

"Because if you keep busy, you won't think about them as much"—Another image appeared as Thomas went on—"and the pain won't seem so real"—her eyes were closed—"they'll seem like dreams of strangers"—her head was shaved—"rather than people we loved more than ourselves"—her lips were purple and skin was completely vacant of color—"but the memories always come back, no matter how deep we try to bury them."

The image vanished and Thomas began to cry, holding his face in his hands and smearing blood across his face. Andrea sat on the opposite side of the hall, thinking over the images of the girl. She didn't look familiar, but for some reason she felt this girl played a large part in not only Thomas's past, but her own.

"Tom . . ." Sobs filled the air. "Tom, who was that?" He continued to cry. "What's her *name*?"

His sobs silenced for a moment, he replied, "Mel."

"Mel who? What's her full name?"

He dropped his hands from his face and looked into Andrea's eyes. "Melissa Pomene."

Pain radiated. Screams of agony filled every corner of every room of the complex as erased memories were uploaded as thoughts from the files Pandora had saved.

Ragnorak

IN THE BEGINNING, THERE WAS DARKNESS. SILENCE ENveloped all sides. There were no thoughts, no memories, no pain—only darkness, creating an eternity of sanctity.

In the distance, light appeared—small, but bright and radiant in a sea of darkness. With each passing moment it pulsated rhythmically, growing in size, slowly devouring the darkness, inch by inch.

Clarity became blinding, peacefulness became confusion, and sanctity became obscured. With its growth and the disappearance of calming serenity, feelings returned. Memories, one by one, were arranged and replaced in order of occurrence, creating a chain of cause, effects, circumstances, and regrets.

With an explosion of awakened senses, reality returned.

✳ ✳ ✳

Footprints of red blood on white tiles blurred and focused into view. Andrea's fist, beating against cold steel, filled Pandora's rooms and hall with sound.

Thomas stared. Fresh blood, matting the hair to the sides of his face, stained his collar and sleeve. He got up and followed the prints leading from pools of blood to Andrea. Movements and sounds wavered in and out of his consciousness as he steadied himself against the wall. Trying to stand, he placed one foot firmly to the ground, pushed up, slipped, and fell back to the floor.

Andrea turned from the hatch to Thomas, one arm hooked loosely across the ladder, the other hanging at her side. Before she could speak, her grip failed, her feet tangled, and she fell to the floor with a loud crack of her skull. The hollow thud of her body hitting the floor drowned out the hum of the generators before white silence settled in.

Neither moved.

Thomas lay on the ground, staring at Andrea's closed eyes and tangled legs. He tried to speak, mouthing words through chapped lips that were barely audible.

First a finger, then a hand, then an arm lifted and fell. Then Andrea moved her legs and allowed them to fall into what looked to be an uncomfortable position. She opened her eyes and straightened her body as best she could before lying back motionless, exhausted.

After what seemed like hours of silence, wavering in and out of consciousness, Thomas accumulated enough saliva to speak. "Anne." He moved a hand, smearing blood from one side of the hall to the other. Using what little strength he had left, he pulled himself toward Andrea. She had yet to move, speak, or open her eyes.

He touched her hand. Her flesh felt cold and vacant of life. He attempted to intertwine her fingers with his own, but couldn't. He grabbed the palm of her hand, only to have her pull it away. She opened her eyes.

"Anne . . ." He attempted to clear his throat. "Andrea? Are you all right?" His words were dry and dense, barely above a whisper.

Andrea did not respond. Instead, she placed one hand to the floor, and with shaky arms and blurred vision, maneuvered her legs in a position to sit completely upright. Winded, she leaned against the wall, catching her breath.

Her face was gaunt, devoid of color. Her lips were purple and chapped. Wheezing, she kept her eyes focused on the opposite wall.

As she caught her breath, Thomas pushed himself upright and leaned back against the wall near Andrea. Both were breathing heavily, staring at the blood-streaked wall opposite, thinking about everything that had occurred since their first encounter with Munin and the Pandora Project.

Placing one hand against the wall and the other into the air to steady her balance, Andrea attempted to stand. Thomas continued to stare vacantly at the opposite wall, speaking with as much clarity as possible. "I think . . . I think I know what happened. I think I know why . . . it erased our memories."

Andrea carefully stepped to the opposite wall.

"Munin said it thinks . . . learns," Thomas went on. "There have been so many here. It learned . . . from the memories. Somehow it's . . . *we're* connected to the system..."

Hand over hand for support, leaving pink palm prints of dried blood, Andrea made her way down the hall.

"We saw each other's memories"—Andrea passed the door to her room—"and it needed something"—and finally reached the kitchen—"and it wouldn't stop . . . until it got it."

She stepped into the kitchen and leaned against the countertop for a moment before reaching for the faucet. Needing water, she turned the handle but nothing happened. She looked at the faucet in shock, unsure of what was happening. She turned the other with the same results. Wanting to scream in frustration, she couldn't find the strength to utter a sound. She lost her balance and fell to the floor as the lights began to flicker. Andrea looked up, searching for a reason to care, and found none.

Thomas leaned in the kitchen doorway.

Between moments of light and darkness, a streak of blood leading from the sink to the pantry appeared and vanished. Using the counter for support, Thomas followed its trail to empty water bottles and Andrea's disheveled body on the floor. She was staring vacantly into a half-empty bottle of water clasped in her right hand.

Unsure of how to proceed, he let gravity take control and fell to the ground, knocking water bottles across the floor. Desperate, he picked up the nearest full bottle, unscrewed the cap, and drained it. The liquid swirled in his mouth and ran down his throat, reviving swollen flesh, dried tongue, and parched throat. When he finished, he dropped the bottle and leaned against the pantry wall beside Andrea, legs spread, gasping for air. His chest heaved with each breath. He wanted more, but he felt like he might throw up.

Andrea didn't move or speak. Her eyes remained focused on the bottle in her hand as the room faded from light to dark. Thomas was analyzing the situation, and what it could mean. "Something's happened." His voice was raspy, but speech came more easily now. "Whatever Pandora needed from us, it got. We need to get to the control room and figure out what's going on."

Thomas moved to stand. Using the floor and wall for balance, he steadied himself on one knee. He reached for Andrea with his free hand.

Her eyes remained fixed on the half-empty bottle in her hand.

He reached for her hand again. She pulled away. "Andrea, we need to see what's going on." He reached for her hand a third time, and again she pulled away. "What's *wrong* with you?" he pleaded.

Her eyes red, cheeks hollow, and hair matted, Andrea turned toward Thomas, his face haggard and beard knotted. His eyes searched for answers and an explanation she was reluctant to give, but uttered nonetheless.

"What happened twelve years ago?" she asked.

"What?" He stared into the creases of her aged face. Her expression remained stoic and unchanged, revealing the explanation. "Andrea . . ."

"Why did we divorce, Tom?"

"We've been through this."

"What happened?"

"I didn't know it was you."

"What did you do?"

"It was an *accident!*"

With each flicker of the fluorescent light, her expression remained still. "And some things can never be forgiven," she said.

Steadying herself against the wall, Andrea dropped the water bottle and tried to stand. Thomas rubbed the back of his head, desperately searching for answers. Still on one knee, he spoke more to the floor than her face. "I didn't know it was you," he said. "I thought it was Melissa."

Andrea stood up straight and attempted to leave. Thomas stood, grabbed her shoulders, and pinned her to the wall.

"We almost died!" he yelled.

Arms limp and face hard, the veins in Thomas's neck throbbed in anger. "Do you also remember how neither of us could control our actions, let alone our thoughts?" he said.

"But you were the only one who——"

He cut her off. "It wasn't rape!" His grip tightened, then quickly relaxed from exhaustion, his hands leaning against Andrea more for support than to keep her from moving.

"Then what was it, Tom?"

His anger began to waver. He searched for an answer that could define his actions as anything other than what she believed they were for the past twelve years.

"It had to have been something," she said. "Was it sex? Making love?" He said nothing. "Fucking?"

"No!"

"Then what was it!"

"It was Melissa!"

Their eyes locked. Faces close to the other. Both were angry, but Thomas felt the need for justification.

"What does that mean?" she asked.

"It means I was making love, but not to you."

Keeping his eyes on Andrea's, Thomas took his hands from her shoulders and stood erect. They stood in the flickering darkness staring at the other. His face softened while hers held onto hatred, sadness, and fear.

"I was making love to Melissa."

His eyes wavered from hers to the wall, then the floor. His body slumped, as if the energy had been drained by the truth of his words. Needing to sit, he moved to the kitchen and pulled out a chair. Resting his forearms on his thighs and facing the door, he stared at the floor in an attempt to make sense of all the chaotic thoughts.

"I didn't know what I was doing. If I could have stopped myself, I would have, but I wasn't here. I was with Melissa . . . on the night she died."

Andrea looked at the wall, expression unchanged. He continued. "We were at the hospital. She'd been admitted for long-term care. And when she wasn't in the hospital, she was staying at my house. She moved in with my mom when she started getting worse and her aunt refused to take her to the hospital when she was sick. She was weak, and the radiation treatments were no longer having the same effect. It was our anniversary, one year to the day, when she agreed to get treatment and I agreed to go to college. It was the only way I could convince her to fight. Unless I went to college, she was going to do nothing but let the cancer slowly eat away at her body until it killed her. She didn't see the point. Looking back, maybe she was right."

Andrea said nothing.

"I was home, finished with the first year of college. I wouldn't have been there otherwise. Part of the agreement was I couldn't miss any classes and had to maintain a 3.8 GPA. If I didn't, she'd stop the treatments. I missed classes, but made up for it with a 4.0."

Thomas smiled. Andrea continued to look at the wall. Neither looked at the other. The smile faded as he continued.

"She was sick—too sick for more treatment. The doctors didn't know how much longer she had, but they knew it wasn't much. A week or two, maybe. We didn't need to tell her. The coughing fits said it all. She knew she didn't have much time, and that was why—"

"She wanted a good —"

"No! That's not it! It was more than that! Much more!"

Thomas turned toward her, shadows from the flickering lights revealing her profile. "Do you know what it's like to know you're going to die?"

"I have an idea."

"Well, imagine knowing for months that no matter what you did, or how hard you fought, it didn't matter. Your body was going to fail you. One by one your organs would shut down until it couldn't take the stress of the unstoppable disease. Now imagine that everyone else knows it too. Doctors, nurses, friends, family, boyfriend, everyone—and they all looked at you differently. They look at you like you're a ghost. They treat you like you're going to break, like you're already dead. That's how people treated her. That's how I treated her. And she was tired of it.

"She didn't want the looks, the special treatment. She didn't ask for it. She just wanted to be normal. It's the reason she refused to tell people about it for so long. She didn't want the feeling of being buried already. She wanted us to be like every other couple without having the stress of sickness and death constantly looming over our heads like a foreboding cloud, even if for just a few minutes. I couldn't deny her that. Could you?"

Thomas stared at Andrea's face, looking for any signs of emotion. He found none.

"So, no—it wasn't sex, or anything else you can think of. It was making love. And it was the last emotion she felt before dying in that hospital room, knowing that the person holding her loved her more than life itself—and I wouldn't have had it any other way."

Frustrated, lost, annoyed, broken, and sick to his stomach, Thomas stood and left the pantry, leaving Andrea standing alone. With one hand on the counter, he carefully avoided the blood on the floor and walked through the open door and into the hall. He turned toward the control room, took two steps, but stopped before he could take a third.

Under failing lights and moments of darkness, Thomas reflected on the reality of everything that had taken place within Pandora's subterranean walls, away from the storm that raged above. The picture of perfection Pandora once was no longer existed. Floors, walls, sheets, clothing—all showed the wear of the years.

Bloodstains marred the floors of the rooms and halls, foot- and handprints circled in and around one another. Flashes of the past did not occur. Memories of lost days, forgotten scents, tranquil moments, and tormented dreams did not come without warning. All that manifested was silence. And with that silence, Thomas returned to the pantry.

Standing in the doorway, Thomas stared at Andrea's profile. She continued to look straight ahead. "I knew what Pandora meant," he said.

Andrea turned toward Thomas. "What?"

"The day Munin gave us the schematics of the complex, I knew the story of Pandora."

Without responding, Andrea turned back to face the wall.

"I didn't know what else to say. I knew that you knew the story of Pandora, and I thought it would be a great way to get you to talk." She remained silent. "I also knew what Lethe meant."

Annoyed, she stepped away from the wall and around Thomas and went into the kitchen.

"It was the River of Forgetfulness in Roman mythology."

She walked through the kitchen, using the counter for support. Thomas called after her. "Andrea . . ." She continued on. "Andrea, I'm . . ." She didn't stop. "Andrea, I'm *sorry!*" She paused.

"For everything, Andrea—Munin, Pandora, Michael, Melissa, me, everything. It's all my fault. I got you into all of this and I'm sorry. I wanted to go back. I wanted . . ." He paused, trying to find the words.

"I wanted to see my dad again and help him work on his motorcycle. I wanted to see Melissa, talk to my mom, be a kid again. I wanted to do it all over, and I'm sorry."

Letting the words hang in the air, Andrea resumed walking.

"What do you want?" Thomas asked, yelling. Andrea stopped in the door of kitchen. She did not turn around. "I know I hurt you, but look around. This is it. How much longer do you think we can last? Why are you acting like this?"

"Why?" she asked angrily, turning around. Thomas's face sagged. "Because none of it's fair! None of it matters! You're right, Tom—this is it. Any minute, Pandora could send us to revisit our broken memories for the last time, but unlike you I won't be forced into a coma from a swollen hippocampus to relive pleasant thoughts of dead loved ones, loving parents, and a happy childhood. I'll be forced into the living nightmare of rape, betrayal, and death. That's my life. I have no happy memories. None. At least none worth remembering."

"That's a lie."

"It's the truth."

"Then what about Michael? What about the day he told you about Romulus and Remus, making you fall in love with astronomy? You may not want to admit it, but I was there with you. I saw the memory, felt the emotions, the wonder, the excitement. You loved what you're brother said."

"My brother is dead."

"So is Melissa. She's not coming back, and neither is Michael. But we still have their memories. It's because of them we're alive today."

"No, it's because of them we're broken. It's because of them we're trapped here, seconds away from death because of a haywire computer intent on completing a futile mission."

Thomas crossed his arms and shook his head. "You don't believe that."

"I don't believe that?" she asked mockingly.

"No. I don't think you do."

Andrea paced a few steps before stopping were she began, looking back at Thomas. "Do you know where I was while you pummeled sex organs into my body and reminisced about making love to your childhood sweetheart?"

Thomas remained silent. Arms crossed.

"I was twelve years old, in the morgue of a hospital, lying next to the dead body of my brother. Do you know what I was wishing for as I lay there in my jacket on that Christmas Eve? I wished that Michael and I had switched spots. That it had been me who died that night, not him. That I had gone flying out the windshield going fifty miles an hour after losing control of the car because of a fast approaching Outage.

I wished the Clouds wouldn't have knocked out the power throughout the entire area, preventing an ambulance from reaching us until a half hour later. But what I wished for most of all was that I wasn't driving. That Mike wasn't teaching me to drive a stick shift. That I didn't single-handedly killed my brother. The one person I ever loved."

Thomas's face washed itself of emotion.

"You took that memory of being with my brother for the last time before burying him, and replaced it with another moment of random sex. After that, I had nothing left. No innocence, no happy memories, just me. So I quit. But I'm sorry. Maybe you want to hear a different story—one that's similar to the one Mike told me when I was a kid, but about your name rather than mine, since you know so much about Roman mythology. Do you know where Charon comes from?"

He said nothing.

"Well, according to mythology, Charon is the name of the aged boatmen who ferried souls across the River of Tarturus to be judged by three deities for their transgressions in life. I knew this before meeting you. It was the reason I started dating you. In fact, it was the only reason we met. Not because I thought you were attractive, or felt some sense of connection. It's because of what your name meant. Congratulations, Tom—you fulfilled your prophecy. The same was true for Professor Loki."

"So you felt nothing for him?"

"No."

"And nothing for me?"

"No."

"I don't believe that."

"Believe what you want." She threw her hands into the air and turned to walk away.

Thomas stood and watched. "Michael's dead," he said.

Andrea stopped. She did not turn to face him.

"And so is Melissa" he went on. "They're not coming back. It's something we're both going to have to live with.

No matter what we do, we can't change the past—no matter how many times we relive our memories. I'm sorry for everything that's happened to you over the years, and I'm sorry for everything I did to hurt you, I truly am, but we can't take it back."

Tears began to stream her face as Thomas continued. "The moments are over, in the past. There's no getting them back. And say what you want, our minds did connect twelve years ago. Although I was making love and you were lying next to your brother, the memories were on the same frequency when Pandora downloaded them to the database. Only they were not of happy memories. They were of people we loved, and how we were never going to be with them again. They were the same emotion and you know it."

Andrea turned to face Thomas with tears in her eyes. "God, Tom, why are you doing this? What is it you want?"

"The same as you. To bring back the people I love. To not hurt anymore. To not wish that I died instead of them. But there's nowhere else we can run." He took a step toward her.

She continued to cry in the center of the kitchen. "You used me," she said.

"I did—and you used me." He took another step closer, his expression calm and trusting.

"You lied to me. You said you'd be there and you weren't. You were supposed to take care of me."

He took another step. Andrea's voice filled the room. "Why did you *lie* to me? Why did you leave?"

Thomas wrapped his arms around her. Without resistance, she placed her head on his chest. Tears soaked into his shirt. "Why did he have to die?" she wept.

He heaved a heavy sigh. "I don't know."

"He wasn't supposed to. He left me alone. He wasn't supposed to leave me alone. I didn't know what to do. What was I supposed to do?"

The question went unanswered as they stood in the center of the kitchen, holding onto each other, Andrea clinging to him as if dying of suffocation.

Minutes passed, neither spoke.

Thomas continued to hold her tight as she held onto him with all her remaining strength, crying. Each silent room was filled with the stains of their broken past. Flickering lights, disheveled clothes, strained faces no longer mattered. All they cared about was their shared warmth, the touch of the other's skin, the awareness that each was as broken and human as the other.

Tears slowed and fists unclenched as they held onto each other, exhausted, awash in clarity.

Andrea removed her hands from around his waist and dried her eyes. Thomas looked down and their eyes met. Neither smiled. Both felt exposed, vulnerable, unsure of what step to take next.

"What now?" she asked.

Before he could reply, flashes of orange, yellow, purple, and white appeared behind their closed eyes in a haze of fast-forwarding incoherent scenes. Sounds, silences, and smells from every scenario overpowered their senses as blinding pain shot through their brains, knocking them to their knees. When they could bear no more pain, it abruptly ended.

Senses settled, colors faded.

They opened their eyes to Pandora's flickering lights and the feeling of fresh blood against their cheeks. Regaining their bearings, they rushed to the control room.

As they entered, the screens across the front of the room went black. Andrea pulled out the seat at her work station and tried to bring up her last calculations, with no success. Thomas went to his monitor and had the same results.

One by one, lights along the console faded, sending the room further into darkness.

"What's happening?" Andrea asked.

"I don't know," Thomas replied.

Faces appeared. All ethnicities, expressions, colors, complexions, and body types trailed one after the other in an endless parade. As each face materialized and faded, waves of incredible pain penetrated their bodies.

Their skin temperature dropped, leaving a feeling of icy pins and needles. Before they froze, the temperature reversed and rose until it was searing. The pain was excruciating, but it wouldn't stop, the sensation of burning flesh penetrating their skin to their bones. As the pain moved from their toes to the tops of their heads, each bone felt as if it had been broken, reset, and healed in a matter of seconds. After their skulls were rejuvenated, the cycle continued as each major organ failed and was restored. It wasn't until their brains were shut down and restarted that they reawakened, coughing and gasping for air.

They opened their eyes to partial darkness from the cool floor. Lights no longer flickered as the complex settled into darkness. The only source of illumination was a green glow from the computer console, displaying the time, day, month, and year.

Dazed, confused, feeling as if they were using their bodies for the first time, Thomas and Andrea felt along the floor. As their eyes adjusted, they were able to make out each other's form in the dimness. Moving slowly, still in pain, both sat up and leaned back against the console. They stared into the darkness of the hall, the blackened rooms, and the closed hatch.

Without turning his head, Thomas spoke, his echo penetrating the silence. "We're still connected to the system. Those images . . . feelings . . . were Pandora uploading its files into the satellite. It's not over."

Head straight, eyes forward, Andrea stared into the darkness. Thomas continued. "The generators are shutting down. As they fail, Pandora dumps a portion of its files."

"How many generators are there?" she wanted to know.

"Three. We still have one more. When it shuts down, the last of the files will be sent, the hatch will open, and it'll be over."

The words circulated throughout the room before fading.

"I don't think I can do that, Tom."

He turned his head toward her, her green-tinted silhouette outlined in the darkness. "What are you talking about?"

"I'm too tired." Her voice began to tremble. Tears ran from the corners of her eyes. "I don't want to do this anymore."

"But we're done. After that generator shuts down, we can go."

"Back to what?" She turned her head and stared into his eyes. "If we walk out and the skies are blue instead of riddled with Clouds, it doesn't change the fact that I'm still alone. It won't bring Michael back. It won't change the past. It won't restore my childhood. I'll still feel lost and lonely. Why should I keep going when so many bad things have happened? There's no point. There never was."

He thought for a moment before responding. "No. Maybe not. But the fact that we keep searching for meaning is what makes us human. It's what makes us flawed. And it's what gives up hope."

In the sanctity of the control room, Thomas Charon and Andrea Remus sat stoic and still beside one another on the floor of Pandora. Eyes softened, expressions relaxed, they looked at each other. Andrea wept and Thomas, smiling, reached for her hand. They interlaced their fingers as the last generators slowly began to shut down, causing the green light of the clock to dim and fade to black. Their eyes remained locked on each other as darkness enveloped them.

With its last ounce of power, Pandora combined day and night into one eternal moment of bliss—flesh firming, wrinkles smoothing, mind and body retreating to that of a child, to be reborn and become an adult again—before shutting down and unlocking its door to the outside world.